DOUBLE DOWN

All In Duet

ISBN-13: 978-0-9997841-5-0

Digital ISBN: 978-0-9997841-3-6

This is book #2 of the All In Duet.

Editors: Madison Seidler, Marion Archer, Natasha Tomic

Proofreaders: Angie Owens, Perla Calas, Erik Gevers

Front Cover Design: Najla Qamber Designs

Front Cover Photography: iStock

ONE

---

dou·ble down

(verb) to strengthen one's commitment to a particular
strategy or course of action, typically one that is potentially
risky.

BELL

I stared at Gwen's body, her twisted foot, her awkward splay of
arms, the pool of blood around her head. Now, she would always be
a stranger to me. Why had she come to my suite? To befriend or
confront me? Would we have gotten along, or would we have hated
each other?

Dario hung up the phone. "You need to leave."

"Why did you tell them that I—"

He held up a hand and lifted the phone to his ear. I wanted to finish the question. I needed to know why he would call the police and tell them that I was dead. It was useless. They'd discover the truth the minute they showed up here. They'd turn her over, see her face, and know that it was Gwen and that Dario was lying. Gwen wasn't some faceless brunette. In addition to being Dario's wife, she was one of the most powerful women in Vegas. They'd recognize her. It was a stupid lie to tell.

Dario spoke into the phone, his voice thickening with a Cajun accent I'd never heard from him before. "I got a girl coming into town. I need you to pick her up at the strip."

I poked him in the chest, hard enough to get his attention. "Stop making decisions and *talk* to me."

He hung up the phone. "You're going to Louisiana."

"For what?"

He reached into his pocket and pulled out a set of keys, working through them and pulling an item off the ring. "Go to the stairwell at the end of the hall and use this to get out."

He held up the small grey button. "Go up four flights of stairs and use the same fob to get into the executive garage at the top."

I huffed out a breath of understanding.

"Take the Phantom and go meet up with one of your bosses. Not at their house, or the casino. Meet somewhere else. Which one would kill to protect you?" He asked the question without a slice of levity, each word weighted in the careful instructions of something deathly important.

My breath shortened as if in preparation for flight. "Either." They would. Either of them, if it was necessary to protect me, would kill someone. I believed it the day I was followed from Ian's, and I believed it now.

"I'm going to text you a number. Call it when you get with one of them." He passed my bag to me. "Is your gun in here?"

I nodded, glanced down at my feet. "I need my shoe. It's..."

I pointed in the direction of the living room, and he stepped forward, his eyes focused on the Nike, not looking at Gwen. *Gwen.* His wife. I felt nauseous.

"Hurry."

I stepped toward him for a hug, a kiss, some form of comfort.

He moved away, gesturing to his shirt, which was smeared with bright red blood. "You can't get her blood on you. And you need to go *now*, before anyone gets here." He stepped toward the house phone and lifted the receiver. I stayed in place. I couldn't leave like this. He was sending me away? To Louisiana? He was telling people I was dead? Someone just tried to kill me and *forensics* was keeping him from kissing me?

Maybe it was more than that. I thought of the way he had fallen to the floor beside her body, calling her name over and over, begging her to wake up. He told her he loved her, told her he was sorry. He had been sorry *over us. We* had done this. "Dario, I'm not—"

"GO." He pointed to the door and glowered at me, his jaw set, eyes hard. "Get the fuck out of here. Go to one of your boys and call the number. *Now.*"

I stepped back, searching his face desperately for love, and was devastated to find nothing. I gripped the Nike, hitched my bag higher on my shoulder, and turned, moving with one socked foot, my gait uneven, my heart breaking as I limped toward the stairwell door.

The key fob worked, the garage easy to distinguish, given the glittering lineup of vehicles. I passed his Bentley, a red Ferrari, a giant truck, and a Mercedes before reaching the Phantom. Dario hadn't given me a key and I held my breath as I tried the door. *Unlocked.* Sliding into it, I saw the key sitting in a small compartment in the dash. Surprised at the lack of security, I started the car. Pulling the belt across my chest, I adjusted the seat and hunched over the steering wheel, carefully rolling out of the spot and moving toward the gate.

I made it through the parking garage without hitting anything, and I relaxed a little once I was off The Majestic's property, the car's tint hiding me from view. I headed north and dialed Rick's number first, glancing at the clock. They'd both be at The House.

Rick answered the phone, and I let out a hard sigh at the sound of his voice. "It's me. I need your help. Something's happened."

Lance spoke in the background, and Rick told him to wait a fucking second, then asked me what was going on. I wrapped my hands around the Phantom's steering wheel and glanced down at the dash. Lifting my foot off the gas, I forced myself to slow down. "I need you or Lance—one of you—to meet me." My voice warbled a bit and I clamped down on the sentence, not yet ready to continue, not if I was about to start blubbering into the phone.

"What's wrong?"

"Nothing." Talk about the biggest lie I'd ever told. I amended the words. "I mean, a lot has happened. I—" *I couldn't go into all of it.* "I need some help getting out of town."

Rick interrupted, telling me to meet him at a used car dealership over on First. He promised to be there in ten minutes and hung up without asking any more questions. I had been right. They wouldn't hesitate to protect me.

My phone chirped and I risked a glance off the road. It was a text from Dario.

--Call 255-432-1673 when you are safe and on the way to the airport. Do what he says.

He? Who was *he*, and what would he have me do?

I spotted the car dealership and pulled into the back, parking next to a new Lexus. There, hidden in the shadows, I put my phone in my lap, knotted my hands together, and waited.

Fuck.

"This is a giant pile of shit." Lance tossed over the words while driving, his H1 rattling along the interstate and taking us out of Vegas. I slumped in the passenger seat and said nothing. Rick, who had taken the backseat, grunted in agreement, his head down, eyes on the navigation of his phone.

It hadn't taken long to catch them up on things. Granted, I hadn't told them everything. I had left out Gwen and Dario's history and the reason for their marriage, but they already knew of her father. Hell, *they* were the ones who had warned me about him to begin with, which was why they were so angry. I wasn't sure who they were more pissed at, Dario or me.

I should have listened to them then. I could have gotten out before my heart took ahold of my head and dragged me into this mess. If I had, Gwen would still be alive and I wouldn't be rattling down the highway at one in the morning, heading for a tiny airstrip in the middle of the desert, following the directions of some wahoo named Laurent.

Laurent had been the one who answered the number Dario had

texted me. *Laurent*. The name sounded like some sort of knight, but the drawl had matched the one Dario had produced ... Cajun.

"I'm telling you, this guy is going to take you into some backwoods cabin and make soup from your hair."

Rick snorted. "Or surround you with pet pigs and make you their queen."

"You're not helping," I growled at them both but couldn't help the tiny smile that forced its way out. The man *had* sounded uncivilized, especially with the accent. But if Dario trusted him, I would too.

Though Dario—the man who had yelled at me to *get the fuck out*—hadn't been anything like the man I'd fallen in love with. He'd been a cold, pissed off, blood-covered, stranger.

Then again, he'd just lost his wife. He'd lost his best friend. He'd dropped to his knees and *crawled across the floor* toward her. I'd been jealous, watching him. How fucked up was that? I'd watched him break into pieces, and *I'd been jealous*. I'd thought about us, and what this meant to our relationship. I didn't think about her, or the fact that a woman had just died. *I only thought of myself*. I flicked my eyes to the road and wondered, if I opened the door and flung myself out, if it would kill me. Not that I had the guts to do it.

"I don't get why he told the police you were dead." Rain started to crackle against the windshield and Lance turned on the Hummer's wipers.

Rick tapped his shoulder. "Turn left at the next road. He told them so whoever ordered the hit would get word it was successful."

"Ordered the hit? This isn't a fucking movie, Rick."

"You got better terminology? That's what it was."

"Unless Hawk killed her himself. Though you'd think he'd recognized his own daughter."

I mumbled at them to both shut up and curled my knees to my chest. Rick was probably right. Which meant that Dario suspected someone in the police department was working for Hawk, or whoever else was the mastermind behind all of this. I remembered our oceanfront dinner, the way he'd lowered his voice when he told me about Gwen's father. *Hawk has zero accountability for his actions and half the police force is in his pocket.*

Lance made the turn. "Not to be a buzzkill, but has anyone considered the possibility that *Dario* hired someone to kill Bell? Or that *he* killed Gwen, then showed up again a little bit later, after B arrived, and acted surprised?"

Lance's words were poison, the sort that tasted bland, then soured into a horrible aftertaste. I wanted to claw at my throat and spit out his words. Instead, I focused on taking a deep breath. Then another.

It was a stupid idea.

Wasn't it? I mean, Dario didn't want to kill me, but he did have access. He'd *begged* me to come to the suite. And from behind, he could tell the differences between us—there was no way he'd mistake Gwen for me. Unless he *wanted* to kill her. Kill her, put on a show for me, and we could be together and live happily ever after.

Only, I had seen him.

Heard him.

Felt him.

His grief had been real and painful. His reaction, the playful smirk he gave me when he walked in, the one that twisted into horror when he saw her—no one was that good of an actor. NO ONE. I had to believe it. I had to believe it, or I couldn't get on this plane.

"No." I swallowed, the word too faint, and tried again. "NO. There's no way."

They exchanged looks, and I saw the doubt between them.

I grabbed Lance's arm, forcing him to look away from the road and at me. "NO. I trust him. I'm not an idiot. He's innocent."

If I was wrong, if this whole thing had been a lie and he'd played me and was planning on killing me... then I was stupid enough to *deserve* death. I'd die in some Louisiana swamp and know that I'd brought it on myself. But then, why involve Lance and Rick?

I wasn't wrong. I was in a horrible mess with a man I couldn't seem to connect with, but I loved him. And he, somewhere among that cold indifference, loved me.

I had to believe that.

TWO

My first hours as a dead woman didn't go well. The plane looked like a crop duster and stopped twice to refuel between Nevada and Louisiana. By the time it landed, it was daylight outside and I was sore, hungry, and exhausted.

I stumbled out of the plane, lifted a tired hand to the pilot, and almost ran into the broadest chest I'd ever seen.

"Easy there." The man held out his arms and stopped me. "You Bell?"

"Yeah." I stepped back and tilted up my head to see him. In the glare of the sun, he was only a large outline, one topped by a baseball cap, with the sort of build that indicated a life built from labor.

"It's a pleasure to meet ya. I'm Laurent." He reached down and grabbed my bag. "This all you got?"

It took me a minute to understand the question, his thick voice rolling the syllables together. I nodded. "Yeah."

"For a dead girl, you sure chatter on." He smiled, his attempt at a joke falling flat. I looked away, and he deflated a bit. "Okay. Let's go."

I turned and watched a fueling tank pull up to the plane. "Is he staying here?"

"Nah. He going to go further on, so any bad guys think you're still on board." He opened the gate to a chain-link fence and held it open for me. "That's why we put you on such a little plane. Just in case someone is watching the skies."

I felt a little comfort at *we*, the word an indicator there was a team effort involved in protecting me. But that reassurance was quickly trumped by the bigger threat in his statement, the reference that someone might be watching aircraft traffic in an attempt to hunt me down and finish the botched job. I looked nervously over the exposed parking lot.

He caught my apprehension and laughed. "Don't worry about anything in Lafayette, girl. I know every mouse that farts in these parts."

Well, that settled everything. Any farting mice come my way, I'd have nothing to worry about.

He nodded at my bag. "Dario said you were carrying?"

"Yeah." I rested a hand on the outside of the canvas, reassuring myself of the gun's weight.

"You won't need it with me. Just keep hold of it for now." He walked over to a battered truck, opened his door and tilted his head to the opposite side, indicating for me to get in.

The truck smelled like the woods, and I fastened my seatbelt and reached for my phone, then realized I didn't have it. "Do you have a phone for me?"

"Yeah. Check da glove box."

I opened the box to find an overflowing mess of receipts, manuals, fuses, and wires. I dug through the contents and finally saw a black plastic flip phone. I pulled it out. "Is this it?"

"Yep." He reached his arm back, rooting around in the pocket behind my seat, then produced a car charger that had to be a decade old. "Battery is probably dead. Best to charge it."

He nodded to the cigarette lighter and shifted the truck into reverse. When he looked over his shoulder, he threw a hand onto my headrest, and I got my first real look at him. Wild and unshaven —he had the sort of beard that started before it was trendy. There must be something in the Louisiana water, because he was as huge and muscular as Dario. He wore a loose-fitting T-shirt, his facial features still hidden behind the brim of his cap and that beard.

I plugged in the phone, watching as a battery symbol flashed on the screen. It was almost dead, and I glanced over at him. "Glad to know you're prepared."

He smirked. "Glad to know that you're grateful. Now, *allons*."

He finished backing up and dropped his hand off the seat, popping the truck into gear. A phone rang, and I watched as he lifted his hip and fished another black flip phone out of his pocket. I tightened my grip on mine and didn't feel so snubbed anymore.

"Hey podna."

The caller spoke and I straightened at the sound of Dario's voice, recognizable despite the muffle. I leaned in a little to try and catch the conversation.

"Your beb, she a pain in the ass."

I didn't know what *beb* meant, but I understood *pain in the ass* just fine. I huffed out a curse and looked out the window, watching the lights of the runway grow smaller. The truck bounced over a rut and I grabbed the handle, holding on.

"I know. Don't worry, brother. I take good care of her." He ended the call and glanced over at me. "He's worried about you. You've got a good man there."

I turned to face him. "Have you known him a long time?"

He laughed, and it was big and hearty. "Oh yes. Me and Dario, we are like brothers. He's a coonass, same as me—though you can't tell it from those suits and da fancy accent he spits."

"Did you ever meet Gwen?"

The smile dropped as quickly as it came, and he watched the road for a long moment before answering. "Nah. I seen her from afar. He didn't like to mix his worlds. And she..." He shook his head soberly. "She had enough evil in her life already. Didn't need no Cajun spirits entering into that. He kept her away from us. Prob'ly good he did."

Cajun spirits. He spoke of them reverently, as if they were real, and a blanket of unease settled over me.

"I'd like to speak to him. Is his number in this phone?" I turned the Motorola over in my hand and opened the top of it, struggling to use the menu.

"Nah. Give the man some time. He's got a lot of fires going right now."

Fires? I thought of the crime scene. Her foot. The blood. What was he telling the police? Did they know I was there, that I found her? My parents popped into my mind and I fought the urge to dial their number, one of the few I knew from heart.

"Let's talk 'bout your rules."

Rules. My back stiffened at the word.

"No talkin' to anyone, other than me. No calling anyone. If that phone rings, you can answer it. It'll be the boss man, checking on you's. But you don't call *anyone*, got it?"

I nod. "Got it."

"I'm serious. No getting yourself killed with *cooyon* shit."

"Cooyon?"

He sighed. "It means foolish, stupid."

On another day, I'd have snapped at him and dialed my parents, then the boys, and maybe my roommates.

But it wasn't another day. I watched the passing of big branched trees that lined the dirt road. His truck slowed and I watched a dog run across the road, his ribs visible, tail tucked. I curled my knees to my chest and thought back to that Vegas suite, and how close I came to dying.

This wasn't a game. I thought I knew that before, had weighed those consequences a week ago, but had I really understood? Right now, my friends would believe that I was dead. My parents. *What would that news do to them?*

If I had been in that suite instead of Gwen, and looked down the barrel of a gun, would I have regretted my love for Dario?

I probably would have. I probably would have stood there and begged for mercy, given him up and promised to never see him again.

Love wasn't worth dying for, not when death could be avoided, not when two souls could part ways and each carry on long and healthy lives.

But we hadn't parted ways and that decision had *killed* her. I stole her husband, then stole her life. I did it all and then ran away, to this cooyon truck, in this cooyon swamp, and regretted it all.

I rested against the seat, closed my eyes, and asked Gwen for forgiveness.

ROBERT HAWK

Robert Hawk walked down the dark hall, his steps confident in the dark. At the room at the end, he opened the door without knocking, pleased to see the thin figure at the window. He stepped inside and stopped, crossing his arms over his chest. "I just spoke to the police. They confirmed Bell Hartley's death."

Claudia turned to face him, and the bedside lamp illuminated the lovely angles of her face. In the half-light, her features relaxed, she reminded him of her mother. Thankfully, that was where their similarities stopped. Unlike Gwen's mother, who had been a majestic and graceful woman, raised in upper-class London, with the fancy accent to prove it, Claudia's mother had been a stripper. Claudia's childhood had been a grab bag of public schools, TV dinners, and cheap clothes. The girl had practically raised herself, navigating through her mother's terrible choices and laziness. If Robert Hawk hadn't stepped in when he had, who knows what sort of worthless individual she might have become.

Now, she smiled, and he could see the pride in her face. "I told you."

"And I told you that I verify everything."

She knew this, of course. She remembered everything, this one. She was diligent. Smart. Obedient. Loyal. And now, as she had proved—capable of solving problems. He smiled at her clean and swift disposal of Bell Hartley. It wasn't the first girl he'd killed to protect Gwen's lifestyle and happiness. Not that the spoiled thing had ever appreciated it. That'd always been her problem. He gave the child everything she wanted, and when he expected Gwen to *sacrifice* for it, to *earn* it, she'd always balked at the actions necessary to achieve the results.

It was the same way with his pets. The girls he kept—they didn't understand that they were being groomed and could be rewarded, based on their performance and respect. Respect was the hardest. You poke a cattle prod in a girl, and she would perform. Spark that baby, and she'd dance upside down on her tits if she could. Performance was easy. Respect ... that was more difficult. Respect without fear, that was almost impossible. Out of twenty-four pets, he'd only had *one* who'd ever learned, *one* who took the lessons as they had been intended. Claudia.

Sometimes he wondered, if he had put Gwen through the same training, would she have shone, as Claudia did—or would she have failed, as all the others had.

He cleared his thought, meeting her eyes. "You did very well. I'm very proud of you."

She swelled with the praise, a small blush coloring those cheeks. In his pocket, his cell phone rang. He pulled it out and smiled when he saw Dario's name. It had taken long enough, seven hours passing since Claudia had returned.

He toyed with the idea of not answering it and making the man wait. Surely, he understood what he'd done. Surely, he knew that Robert was responsible for taking his fuck toy from him. His grin widened. Surely, Dario was furious.

Maybe this would be the moment when Dario's temper was finally displayed. He'd felt hints of it, seen a few sparks of fury, but had never had the chance to watch it explode. It seemed a pity to experience it through a phone.

His anticipation got the best of him and he pressed the button and answered the call. "Dario." His exuberance slipped through the name, and he couldn't help but inject warm affection into the next question. "To what do I owe this pleasure?"

When Dario spoke, his words were tightly controlled wedges of dynamite. "I'm outside. I suggest you open the front door before I break it in half."

Hawk straightened to his full height, his grin widening.

This. This would be fun.

THREE

DARIO

Dario's fury flexed, his grief and anger mixing into a cocktail he fought to contain. Now was the time to stay calm and be smart.

The ornate door swung open, revealing the opulent interior. Robert Hawk squinted at him. "It's early, Dario. You're lucky I wasn't in bed."

"I wasn't aware the Devil had to sleep."

The old man barked out a laugh, his eyes gleaming. If Dario was right, if he had set up Bell to die, he certainly wasn't feeling any remorse.

"Come in, son. You seemed upset on the phone. Night not going your way?" He stepped back, waving off the suits behind him. Dario assessed the security detail. Two large men with guns on their hips, both carrying the sort of dead-eyed allegiance that money bought. If need be, he could take them, but he'd risk death in the process.

Hawk moved into a sitting room and took a high-back chair, one built for grandeur over comfort. "Well?" Hawk raised his eyebrows and couldn't—or didn't try to—control the glee on his face. Soon, he wouldn't be so happy. Soon, once he found out about Gwen, he would implode.

Dario cleared his throat and forced his words to come out in as calm a manner as possible. "A couple of hours ago, I received a call from the police. There's been an incident at The Majestic."

"I can't be bothered regarding every little incident that occurs, Dario. Surely you're a big enough boy to handle these sorts of things by yourself."

"I'm here because I suspect you had a part in this."

The man all but preened, his legs crossing, one hand reaching up to run through his thick mop of white hair. Dario imagined him scalped, that patch of hair hanging from his grip, the blood dripping from it.

"I have a part in *everything* that goes on in my casinos."

"Including murder?"

Hawk shrugged. "If the situation calls for it."

Dario walked over to the row of bookshelves, his steps measured, eyes flicking over to the bodyguards, who flanked either side of the door. He eyed the shelves, which held an assortment of collectibles and first edition books. He reached forward, picking up a Getty bust and examining the deep lines in its face, the dead look in its eyes. Hawk revered the man. Dario had sometimes wondered if he hadn't left his daughter at the mercy of Mexican kidnappers in an attempt to emulate the man. Only, Gwen hadn't lost an ear. She'd lost so much more.

"I don't engineer situations, Dario. I respond to them. Just like I respond to disloyalty."

Dario waited for him to continue, to confess something, but the old man stayed silent. He set down the bust and carefully chose his next words. "You think disloyalty should be punished?"

"I think you're talking in circles when you seem to have an accusation to make."

Dario moved further down, circling the end table, until he was back in the man's line of sight. He stopped, his hands in his pockets, and met his gaze. "I want to know why you had her killed."

"Ah. I *thought* I heard something about a woman dying. A brunette, right? But surely you don't think I had anything to do with that."

"I think you had everything to do with it."

The man's mouth curved a little at the sides, a gruesome half-smile forming. "As I said before, I have a part in everything that goes on in my casinos. *My* casinos. Not yours. Just like Gwen. Gwen is not yours, she's mine. And you haven't been treating what's *mine* with the right level of care."

The urge to smash his head against the table, to break his neck and rip his body into pieces... it was too great and Dario forced himself to take a moment. He sat behind the heavy oak desk and pulled open a drawer. "I need a drink. You have a fucking drink in here somewhere?" He slammed the drawer.

"I'm intrigued to see that you're so affected by this woman's death, Dario. It disappoints me, to say the least."

The second drawer of the desk was half open when Hawk spoke. Dario paused, his hand inside the drawer, before pulling his hand back out. Slowly rising to his feet, he pushed the drawer closed with the toe of his shoe.

Walking forward, he halted before the man and lowered himself until he was crouching, their eyes level with each other.

One of the guards protested, and Robert Hawk waved him off. "Let the man speak."

"I *am* affected by her death. I want you to look into my eyes and *see* how affected I am. I want you to look into my eyes and know that I loved her. I still love her. I cherished her. And I cared for her. I broke my fucking back bending over to care for her."

"Be careful Dario. Every word you speak is a spit—"

"Shut up, old man."

The goon's hands closed on Dario's arms, yanking him to his feet and pulling him backward. When Robert Hawk rose to his feet, his face was hard, his eyes glowering, and he stalked forward with the gait of a younger and stronger man.

"You act surprised. Why? You disrespected me by sleeping with that trash. You disrespected my daughter by keeping a mistress. You have gotten too big for yourself, Mr. Capece. I removed the distraction. I righted the ship. You should bow forward and thank me for putting you in line and punishing your slut—something that you didn't seem strong enough to do yourself."

"You didn't right the ship. You sunk it. You think you punished my slut?"

"That bullet did. I heard she sank to her knees like a whore when it hit."

"No." Dario yanked his arms free from the men and glared back at Hawk, the fury and emotion leaking out of the corners of his words. "That was your *daughter* that sank to her knees. That was your *daughter* that the bullet found. That brunette you are so fucking cheery about dying? That was Gwen."

The reaction rippled off Robert Hawk in stages. First came a tremor. The edges of his beard trembled, his eyes narrowed, and Dario watched as his gnarled hands tightened into fists. "Excuse me?"

"Your man killed the wrong woman. He killed Gwen."

Hawk opened his mouth and wiped a trembling hand over his beard. As he swallowed, his Adam's Apple bobbed. "I was told that the Hartley girl was dead. It was verified."

Dario shook his head. "Your source was wrong. I saw her. Held her body. Unless he killed both of them, he got the wrong girl." He pulled out his phone and flipped through the photos, his heart tightening when he got to the one he had taken of Gwen. Taking a deep breath, he held up the phone and let Hawk see the image.

At the sight of her body, his eyes flared, the famous Hawk temper emerging. His hand jerked out, latching around Dario's throat and squeezing. The air supply cut off and Dario's chest seized, his phone dropping to the floor and clattering across the wood. Dario reached up and wrapped his hand around Hawk's wrist. It'd be easy to rip it free. He was ten times stronger than the old man. But he let him have this moment.

"*You* did this!" Hawk's voice broke, his fury and pain mixing together in a cocktail of rage. "You and your swinging dick put my little girl—" His words broke off, and he abruptly released his grip on Dario and turned away.

Dario inhaled deeply, the spots in his vision clearing, Hawk's blurry outline sharpening as the man stopped before the desk. "You can blame me all you want, but this is on *you*. You left her in that fucking Mexico shithouse to die, and you've been killing her ever since. This? This is just the final swing of your ax."

"You cheated on my daughter. You—"

"I LOVED your daughter. I loved her more than you ever did. I did *not* cheat on Gwen. I was honest with her. We were honest with each other. Our marriage, despite what you may have thought, wasn't sexual and it wasn't exclusive."

"Bullshit." The man spit out the word. "Don't try to make excuses to me, Capece. I gave you the world and you shit all over *it*, and all over your marriage." He whirled around and pointed to Dario. "Search him."

THE DOOMED

Through the crack in the open door, Claudia watched, her breaths short and fast, her panic and guilt escalating with each word out of Robert Hawk's mouth.

Dario was lying. He had to be. She had shot Bell. She had to have shot Bell. She couldn't have... she felt suddenly lightheaded and pulled away from the view, leaning against the closest wall.

Dario had shown him a photo, something that had caused Robert to react, to believe that Gwen was dead. Could she be? Could Claudia have actually ... her vision tunneled and she circled her waist with her hands, frantically rubbing her clothing, pulling and stretching at the cotton without thought of why.

She had to go see Gwen. Prove the ridiculousness of this all. Prove that Dario was lying. Claudia was right. Claudia had killed BELL. She'd watched her sink to the floor. She had watched Gwen for years and Bell for weeks. She would have been able to tell the difference between the two glossy-headed brunettes. She would never have made *that* mistake.

She stepped away, her ankle turning, and she grabbed at the wall for balance.

She killed Gwen. It had to be a lie, but the mere possibility of it terrified her. If she killed Gwen, she might as well die now. The thought of Robert's reaction... she made it to the end of the hall and turned left, moving past a housekeeper and quickening her steps, the back door ahead.

She had to go to Gwen. Find her. Prove that this was all a lie.

And if it wasn't?

She pushed on the door, the night quiet, the garage just ahead, her car inside. She stopped, taking a moment to think, fear pricking at the edges of her consciousness. Her car, like all Hawk vehicles, had a tracker on it. Stepping into the shadows, out of the view of the security camera, she reached into her pocket and pulled out her cell phone. Dumping it in the closest potted plant, she hugged the edge of the home until she got to the front, darting past Dario's Rolls and through the front gate.

In case he was telling the truth.

In case Gwen was dead.

In case Claudia killed her...

In case, in case, in case, in case...

She'd have to be smart about this. She broke into a run, her hands fisting into nervous grips. If Dario was telling the truth, her life was over.

DARIO

Dario put up a half-hearted struggle, his arms held tight by the two men, their hands patting over his body. When they pulled at his shirt collar, he stilled, closing his eyes when they undid the top buttons of his shirt and exposed the small mic and wires, taped to his stomach. Hawk spotted them and began to laugh. "Oh... what a stupid, stupid man."

Dario stayed quiet as they ripped the tape off of his chest, following the wires down to the small recorder. It didn't matter. The wire was, always had been, a decoy—something designed to be found and used for distraction.

"Does it have a transmitter?" Hawk asked the closest suit.

The big man picked up the tiny recorder and peered at it. "Nah. Flashdrive."

"Destroy it." He stepped forward until he was face to face with Dario. "Did you really think you'd be able to use that against me? I am too smart for you Dario. And you... you are a man with too big a dick and too small a brain."

Hawk stepped forward, and Dario imagined killing him. Would he cry for mercy? Groan out an apology? A curse? Whatever it would be, Dario would show no mercy and ignore any apology.

He should have killed him years ago. He'd brought it up on dozens of occasions, all rebuked by Gwen, her stern admonishments making him swear to leave the man alone. Now, her blood still fresh in his memory, he regretted every promise. On their wedding night, he should have looked into his eyes, sliced the throat of the bastard, and watched the devil die.

Now, it was too late and Gwen was the one who had taken the punishment. The only one, among the three of them, that was innocent. He didn't know if it was more cruel to let her father suffer in guilt or kill him now. From the mad look on his face, it was impossible to tell if the guilt had hit. The man seemed immune to blaming himself for anything.

Hawk watched as they crushed the recorder, then passed it to him. Tossing it in the general direction of the desk, he turned back to Dario. "Doesn't seem like you, Capece."

Dario shrugged. "Maybe I record all of my conversations with you."

The man laughed, genuinely amused by the comment. "Now, where is the Hartley girl?"

Dario shook his head. "I haven't found her yet. She ran."

"I find that hard to believe. That little wisp of a girl? Running away all by herself?" His face calmed, his emotions clamping under control, and he'd never been so chilling. "Surely, she had some help."

Dario stared him down and wondered what the old man planned to do. Maybe he'd have Dario taken away and torture him for information on Bell's location. The man would take out all of his anger and guilt on Dario, with little concern or fear of the consequences.

Or maybe... he watched Hawk lift a heavy bronze Remington sculpture from the desk, hefting it between his hands as if testing the weight. Turning back to Dario, he raised his hands, the bronze horse straining the cords in his thin forearm.

Dario stared into Hawk's hate-filled eyes and regretted never killing this asshole. Regretted playing along with his games, and letting him dictate every year of his marriage. Without him, Gwen could have married someone for love and not protection. She would still be alive. He and Bell could have been happy. And Dario could have—

Hawk raised the horse above his head. He lunged forward and Dario yanked one arm free and twisted to the side, grappling with the two men as Hawk swung the sculpture down, the sharp tip of the horse's tail aimed at Dario's head.

FOUR

DARIO

Dario slammed his foot into the knee of the goon behind him and the sculpture swung by, close enough that he felt the wind of its wake, and Hawk's arm brushed against his chest.

"Hold him, Goddamn you!" Spittle flew from Hawk's mouth, and he lifted the small statue a second time. His movement froze at the loud and distinct sound of the front door knocker. There was a second rat-a-tat-tat that was quickly followed by a pound against wood.

One of his men appeared in the doorway. "It's the cops."

Hawk's eyes flipped to the wire, then snapped back to Dario. "You rat."

Dario allowed himself a breath, a moment of hope, and spoke evenly. "They're probably here to tell you about Gwen."

A flash of pain showed on Hawk's face, a fleeting peek at the human that must exist somewhere underneath all of the evil.

"Drop him." He pointed to Dario. "Keep your fucking mouth shut."

Hawk looked down at the bronze horse, still hanging by his side and stepped to the desk. Carefully setting it down, he pulled his suit into place and ran a hand through his hair. "Let them in."

BELL

"You too skinny." Laurent stuck a forkful of food in his mouth, and I looked over in annoyance.

"I'm not too skinny."

"You are. Come and eat. You'll like it." He was standing in front of a plate and working through the contents with the efficiency of a competitive eater.

"I'm not hungry." I walked around a saggy recliner and went to the window, trying to see through a year's worth of grime.

"Who you looking for?"

I didn't even know. It wasn't as if Dario was going to show up here. I reached back and touched the cell phone in my pocket, reassuring myself of its existence. It hadn't made a sound so far, no texts or calls, no indicators of Dario's actions. *What was he doing? Did the police still think I was dead?*

"You got too many thoughts going in that head of yours. Come here." He pointed to the opposite side of the kitchen counter. "I'll fix you some jambalaya."

I shook my head. "I'm good. I'm just tired."

"You slept all morning. It's noon. Time to eat."

I'd flown through the night. You'd think the man would cut me some slack, but he was acting as if I was the laziest person alive. "I only got four or five hours of sleep."

He clicked his tongue. "*Pauve ti bite*. Poor little thing."

I flopped down on his sofa, and it shifted from the impact. I stared up at his ceiling and noticed the dust on his ceiling-fan blades. The guy needed to learn how to use a paper towel and some 409. He thought I was lazy? I had opened his fridge last night and saw milk that expired two *weeks* ago.

"You starve to death, Dario's going to be real mad at me."

"I'm not going to starve to death." I turned my head and looked at him. "Is there a plan? How long am I supposed to be here?"

He shrugged as if unconcerned, but he couldn't be pleased to have a sudden and sullen houseguest. I kicked my foot up on the arm of the ancient leather sofa and noticed I was still wearing his socks— mine had gotten wet when I stepped into a puddle between Laurent's truck and his house—a wool pair that was way too big for me, the heels of them bulging out from my ankle in an odd fashion.

I tugged on the bottom of my shirt, the same one from last night. *I could have died in this shirt*. "Do you have any clothes I can borrow? Or can we go buy some?"

He looked up, eyeing me as if gauging my size. "My sistah is too big, but she could loan you something."

His sister. I tried to imagine the sister to this huge and hulking behemoth. I glanced around the room. "Don't you have a girlfriend or ex? Someone who's left clothes here at some point?"

He looked at me as if I was crazy, as if we didn't leave clothes behind like property markers claiming territories.

"I don't have a girlfriend. And you asked 'bout a plan." He brought over a plate of steaming jambalaya and set it down on the coffee table. I sat up, my stomach growling out of habit. "The plan is, we wait for the boss man to tell us what da plan is."

That sounded like a stupid plan. In movies, that sort of plan always caused the sitting ducks to be killed. I voiced my opinion and he chuckled.

"Nobody being kilt on my watch. I keep Dario alive for twenty-five years in that crazy city of his. You on Benoit land here. Nobody going to come o'er here and kill you. Trust me on dat."

I did trust him. It seemed reasonable to feel safe in the middle of the swamp with a man who seemed capable of breaking an alligator in two.

He pushed the plate toward me. "Here. Eat. After that, we can get you some clothes."

I eyed the plate for a long moment, then reluctantly picked up a fork and began to eat.

FIVE

DARIO

The study, which had felt crowded with Hawk and his two men—
was now quickly filled with police officers. "Mr. Capece, if you
could come with us." One of the policemen stepped forward and
put a hand on Dario's shoulder before cuffing his hands behind him.

Robert Hawk straightened to his full height. "Why are you
arresting him?"

"May we speak to you in private, Mr. Hawk? I'm afraid we have
some news to share with you."

Hawk's gaze popped from Dario to the detective, and indecision
broke the rigidity of his features.

"It's about your daughter."

The knot in the middle of Hawk's throat bobbed, and Dario
watched as he ran both hands over the top of his hair, smoothing
down the thick silver strands. "Go on."

"Mr. Capece?" The second uniform gestured to the door, and Dario flexed his hands, not appreciating the feel of the handcuffs, biting into the muscle of his wrists. It had been a long time since he had been in handcuffs. The last time had been twenty years ago, when he had been caught crawling in Mandi Breitlen's bedroom window. Her father had chosen to call the authorities rather than face the fact that his daughter wasn't the angel he thought she was.

"Let's go. We'll read you your rights outside."

Dario followed the man through the door. He stepped out of the house, his eyes drifting over the trio of police cars. They'd certainly cut things close. Another thirty seconds, and he'd be dead. He was brought to a stop next to one of Hawk's men.

"Dario Capece, you are being arrested for the murder of Gwen Capece. You have the right to remain silent. Anything you say can..."

He stared at the pebbled drive, tuning out the Miranda warning, and prayed like hell all of this would work.

BELL

I was only a dead woman for a short time.

I hugged my knees to my chest and watched the small box television, watching as Dario was led through a crowd of reporters and into the jail. Even in handcuffs, he was powerful. Those broad shoulders straight, his head high, his stride confident. But in his face, I saw the strain. In those fierce features, the scowl across those delicious lips... his eyes looked weary. He looked away from the cameras, and I noticed the rough mess of his hair, the limp crease of his expensive collar.

"He looks bad." The comment came from Laurent's sister, a six-foot-tall Amazon with wild curly hair and green eyes that matched her brother's. Septime had all but barreled into the house several hours ago, shoved me aside on the couch, and gave me a look that screamed to toughen the hell up.

We hadn't, in the hours since, become any better friends. A headline appeared below Dario's image, one that matched the broadcasters' chatter.

DARIO CAPECE CHARGED IN WIFE'S MURDER

"You don't think they're going to bring up—" Septime's words fell off abruptly, and I turned just in time to see a look passed between her and her brother. He shook his head minutely, and I straightened up off the couch.

"What? You don't think they're going to bring up ... what?"

"Nothing." Laurent's sister leaned forward, watching the news, and didn't look my way. I turned to Laurent, who met my gaze in the bored manner of a man with a secret. I sank back against the cushion and tried to control my anger. This wasn't fair. They were arresting Dario who wasn't—couldn't be—guilty. I had been there. I had seen his reaction. And now, these two were keeping something from me. Everyone seemed to be keeping something from me.

I crossed my arms tightly over my chest and watched as Dario stopped just before the door to the police station. He turned his head, the camera zooming in as his eyes connected with the lens.

There.

I was sure he was staring at me. I had to believe that there was a promise of security in those eyes. *For us.* I wanted to believe in that connection. He had told me to trust him. He had told me every-thing would be okay.

It was a momentary moment, potentially an imagined promise, but I believed it.

"He didn't do it. You know that."

I ignored Septime's comment, holding Dario's gaze until a navy suit pushed at his shoulder, and Dario turned and passed through the door. Out of sight, but fully protected. Surely, he'd be safe in there. Surely, with all of the uniforms, the guns, the security ... he wouldn't get hurt.

"Don't you be worried 'bout him." Laurent heaved to his feet and reached for the remote, turning the television off. "Our boy has a plan. He always do."

If he'd had a plan, Gwen wouldn't be dead, and I wouldn't be in this dank shack in the middle of the swamp. I swallowed the thought and looked down at the hem of my new shirt, pulling at the cotton.

A timer went off in the kitchen, and Septime lifted her head, pushing to her feet and moving toward the sound. I looked at Laurent, and he tilted his head toward the porch. "Let's go for a walk."

I hadn't walked through the woods in years, not since I was a little girl exploring the forest on the edge of our trailer park. I mentioned this and Laurent laughed.

"Not much else to do but explore. It's probably why we all end up with so many kids."

I had to blush at the thought, though he and Septime were both, as far as I could tell, single. I said that and he shrugged, pushing his hands into the pockets of his jacket.

"Yeah, well. We da picky ones."

He nodded toward a dirt path through the trees, one large enough for a car. Everything was wet from this morning's rain and I pulled my hair into a knotted ponytail, the summer humidity thick in the air.

"A girl died once. At Dario's casino, over in Biloxi." Laurent glanced sideways at me. "That's what Septime was trying to bring up."

My heart fell at the same time that my body did, my foot sinking into a soft spot and causing me to tilt forward, my arms wind-milling through the air as I attempted to stay upright. Laurent reached out, catching me, and I fell against his chest, my hands hooking into the fabric of his jacket as I sagged in his arms. "Shit."

"It's okay, chere."

He lifted me clear off the ground and stepped to the side, eyeing the soft dirt, then set me down, watching as I tested my ankle. It wasn't injured, but my tennis shoe was covered in dark mud. When I took a forward step, things squished around my sock. I made a face. "Crap. There's mud in my shoe."

"That a problem?"

A day ago, I wouldn't have been able to understand him, but I picked through the Louisiana accent without trouble.

"Let me just take it off."

I found a sturdy looking tree and leaned against it, working off my shoe and hitting it against the trunk, wet mud splattering off it.

Laurent made a sound somewhere between a growl and a sigh. "Water will do a betta job."

I broke a stick off the closest branch and tried to scrape a clump out of the sole.

"I'll just carry you."

"No, I'm—" I grunted when he lifted me, fireman style, and flung me over his shoulder. "STOP." I pushed at his shoulder. "Put me down!"

"Hold onto ya britches. I'm just taking you to the creek."

I struggled another moment, then gave up, hanging like a limp rag over his massive shoulders, my arms bouncing against him. I held the muddy shoe in one hand and watched the muddy path sway before me. *A girl died once. At Dario's casino, over in Biloxi.* Had there always been so much death everywhere? Or did it just follow Dario? I spoke to him over his shoulder. "How did the girl die?"

He veered to the right, moving off the road and down a trail. He didn't slow, and I watched his steps, my upside-down angle giving me a front-row view of the carnage his boots made across the fallen leaves.

"She jumped outta the window of one of the suites. Her daddy tried to say that it was from a broken heart."

My stomach rolled, an uneasy movement that could have been caused by my position or his words. "She was dating Dario?"

He shifted me as if I was a bag of flour, putting me in a new position on his shoulder, and I wheezed a little in protest.

"She was dating a lot of men. Dario had been one of them. And he had stopped with her due to the Vegas woman coming into town."

The Vegas woman. Gwen. I pushed against his back just to raise my head, the blood rushing back into place, the woods bobbing around us. I could hear the faint sound of water, and I turned my head, saw the glint of a reflection through the trees. He took another ten paces and stopped, depositing me down with enough care that I thanked him.

"The water's clean, but it's cold."

I carefully hopped to the side, sitting on the edge of the stream and pulling off my dirty sock. As I rinsed it, and my shoe, I thought over what he'd said.

"Do you think she killed herself over Dario?"

"Who knows. Da media, they was all over him for it. Would have probably said he pushed her, but he'd been at dinner with da Hawk girl when it happened. And the security footage showed that there'd been nobody in that suite with her. Suicide, that's what it'd been. And you can't blame nobody for dat."

I watched the water swirl around the shoe and thought about Dario. Thought about how I'd feel if Gwen had come to town, and Dario had dropped me. What had it been like? Had she been a fling of his?

I thought of his dancer and his mistress—the way he'd ended things with them when he had started dating me. I had never considered their reactions, had never thought about how cold my world would suddenly feel if Dario turned his attention away.

In his light, under his attention, everything felt warm and alive and sexually free.

But in this sweaty Louisiana town, with this strange hulk of a man beside me, and Dario in jail ... I was starting to feel the chill of being without him.

SIX

THE RUNNER

In a city of almost a million people, it should have been easy to hide. Moving on foot, through Robert Hawk's gated neighborhood, had been her first challenge. She'd jogged along the treeline, when the first police car had turned down Robert's street. The sight of it had caused her to trip, her shoe snagging on the dirt as she had ducked down and in between two trees. The car had continued on, followed by three more sedans and an armored van.

She'd watched them pass, her alarm turning into confusing. Were they looking for her? The group of blue and whites took a left and turned down Robert's street. *Maybe they were coming for him.* If they showed up ... if he had killed Dario ...

She had shifted her weight from foot to foot, looking back in the direction of the house, then forward, toward the exit. Then, she had continued to run.

Now, huddled over a book in a crowded Barnes and Noble off

Rampart, she worked through every minute of that night. Using the master key Hawk had given her to gain access to Bell Hartley's suite. Waiting in the closet. The tall brunette walking in. Could it have been Gwen?

No. She'd watched her too many times. Memorized every expression she carried, the gracious way she dipped her head, how she navigated easily in heels, each moment fluid and graceful. She'd spent hours in her room, practicing, striving for the seductive yet classy gait that Gwen so effortlessly pulled off.

This woman ... well, she'd been in tennis shoes. Claudia struggled to remember the last time she'd seen Gwen in anything other than heels. Once, on her way to the plane, heading for the ranch. She'd worn tennis shoes then—but she'd been carrying coffee and wearing a long coat, aviators covering half her face. To compare her gait with the woman from the room...

She closed her eyes tightly, her mind bombarded with images. The woman—Bell—slumping to the floor, her hair a mess of gore and brains. Bell. It *had* to be Bell. The awkward sprawl of her limbs. A twitch of her leg. Blood, a pool of it spreading.

She'd seen death before. First as a terrified observer, starving and handcuffed, on the hard concrete floor of a cell. Then, as Robert Hawk's right hand.

But causing death had been a different experience, one that had given her such a dizzying sense of power, of self-pride, of accomplishment. She'd stood over that body and anticipated Robert's reaction, had anticipated sitting across from Gwen and bonding with her.

All those thoughts, those possibilities... she had taken them from herself. Taken Robert's daughter away from him. Left them both alone.

He would be... her mind stalled. *Furious* was not strong enough of a word. There was no word for the pain that he would feel. The fury. The reaction. She could feel a twist of all of it in herself, the self-hatred that burned through her chest.

Had she actually *killed* Gwen?

She dropped her head back and, in the middle of the crowded store, screamed.

DARIO

Dario rubbed his wrists and scowled at the man. "You were a bit rough with the cuffs."

"Hey. Had to make it look authentic." The detective, one of the few clean cops in the department, and one who'd known Dario since his first year in Vegas, leaned forward. "I've got a cell in solitary confinement for you. You want out for a night, you let me know. But I can't have that pretty mug being photographed while you're supposed to be locked up. So be smart and camp out in there as long as you can."

He pushed the open folder across the desk. "This is what we got so far. Eight missing girls. They've disappeared over twenty years, so it hasn't been very high on our radar. I swear, he waits until we're in the middle of a management turnover to take them."

Dario looked at the first page, the girl smiling out from a photo at the upper corner. He recognized the setting. It was an employment photo, the sort The Majestic's HR department took on a new hire's first day, the casino's uniform still stiff, the makeup subdued, the image printed on a shiny card with a barcode and access stamp.

He flipped to the second set of clipped pages. This one was a blonde. Another employee photo, from one of their smaller casinos, Jahar.

Both girls had favored each other. Both pretty. Both young. Both beautiful. Both... just like Bell. The thought made him queasy. He looked back at the photo, sensing a more probable connection. Both girls looked like younger versions of Gwen. And just like Gwen, they were dead. He voiced his thoughts, and the detective shifted in his desk chair.

"Well, now. We don't *know* that they're dead."

Dario lifted his head, breaking eye contact with the third woman's photo. "Excuse me?"

"That one right there?" The man leaned forward, his finger moving to and tapping on another beautiful young girl's photo. "That's Claudia Vorherz. She disappeared two years ago. We thought, her family thought, hell—*everybody* thought she was a goner, just like the rest of them. Same MO to the tee."

He started to check off the items on his short, thick fingers.

"Hawk casino employee."

"Single."

"No family close by."

"Disappeared without any cell phone usage, credit card spending, or packed bags."

The suspense was painful. Dario gave a curt nod. "And?"

"And ... then she showed up eight months ago. Alive, fit as a fucking fiddle, not a scratch on her—at least, not anywhere her mother could see."

This hadn't hit the news. He pinned the man with a hard look. "And why the *fuck* have you not shared this with me before?"

Each girl that went missing had produced massive media coverage, police investigations, the questioning of employees ... and each one had been hell on Gwen. With each disappearance, she'd spent weeks in alcohol and medication-fueled depressions, the downturns only cured by time and—eventually—trips to the ranch. Solo trips that brought her back with flushed cheeks, glowing skin, and peace in her eyes.

If she had known that one of the missing girls had *survived*, had been fine... he fought the urge to flip over the detective's desk in frustration.

The man leaned back as if sensing the possibility and spread his hands in surrender. "We didn't want to lose momentum. With the girls spread so far apart, we were already having trouble keeping the media—and our chief—focused on finding their abductor. Or killer. Or whatever this guy is."

"*This* guy? It's Robert Hawk. No question."

"Well, yes. That's what we suspect."

Dario growled underneath his breath. The man responsible was Hawk. There wasn't a doubt in his mind of that. But he could understand the police department's reluctance to put that label on him. After all, he was one of the most powerful men in Vegas. A close friend of the governor and a major contributor to his re-election fund. Hell, Hawk had sponsored the police department's Christmas dinner this year, in addition to his generous annual scholarship program for law enforcement children.

"But suspicions aren't enough to get a warrant. We need something concrete on him. You know that."

Yes, Dario had known that. It was why he'd spent the last five years secretly helping. He'd worked with the detective to set up office phone taps, had fed them information about Hawk's schedule, his habits, his real estate holdings and shell corporations. He'd given them a hundred clues, and they hadn't found jack shit tying Hawk to the missing girls.

"You've got the recording from today." While the wire crudely taped to his chest had been as easy to find as a crack whore behind Jerry's Nugget, the real transmitter, a bug the size of a piece of popcorn, had gone undetected. It was still right where he'd left it, behind the Getty bust.

"The recording implicates him on Gwen, not these girls." The man gestured to the row of photos.

"Then arrest him for Gwen. Now." He needed Hawk locked up. Precious time was ticking by, considering Bell was at risk every day that Robert Hawk walked free. The moment Hawk had learned she was still alive… she'd been back in danger. It was a necessity he hated, but one that was inevitable. Gwen's death was a secret with a very short shelf-life, especially with the number of moles in this department.

"Be patient, Dario. We'll arrest him. But we have to be smart about it or you know what'll happen. We'll bring him in, question him, and then his lawyers will pick apart every line of that tape until it looks like a kindergartener's lunch plate. They'll have him out on bail and he won't make another mistake, not in the months before a trial."

He was right. It was why the plan was to tail Hawk and wiretap his home and cell phone. Let him blow up about Gwen and lead them to the man he'd hired to kill her. If there was anything Dario knew, it was that Robert Hawk did not allow a misstep to go unpunished. And the death of his only daughter? He would bring the wrath of God down on that individual.

Dario took a pained breath, his heart still raw at the realization that Gwen was dead. Gone. *Forever*. His Gwen. She'd never smile at him over coffee. Would never know that Claudia Vorherz was safe.

Would never slip her hand into his and affectionately squeeze his palm.

Dario stared down at the third girl and struggled to maintain his composure. *Claudia.* "So, what did she say? This one?"

The man shrugged. "We couldn't get to her in time. She showed up at her mom's house on Christmas Day, as if everything was hunky-dory. Brought her a present, as if seeing her wasn't enough. Stayed there four hours, didn't tell her dick about where she'd been for nearly a year and a half, then crawled out a window and left."

"Why'd she crawl out a window? Why didn't she just walk out the door?"

"My guess? She didn't want to answer any questions about when she'd see her again."

Dario looked at the page, his eyes skimming over the details of her disappearance. The detective was right. Everything about her fit the profile, down to the sunny smile on the brunette's photo. A smile that made him think again of Bell. A pull of longing snuck past his grief. Earlier, after she'd laid down to sleep, Laurent had called. The small details of her day had made him yearn for the humid air of the swamp, the tiny shack that Laurent owned, the taste of gumbo and fried gator tail. He'd have loved to show her that life, to tell her stories of his youth, and laugh over her reactions. Another opportunity missed, stolen from their progression as a normal couple.

Dario looked back down at the file and tried to retrace his thoughts. "How long ago was that? And no one's seen her since?"

"About six months ago. And yep, no one's seen her since. It really let the air out of our investigation. Hell, maybe all of them are runaways."

They weren't. Dario could feel it in his bones, knew the potential in

Hawk's evil, had seen the evidence of it—just one day ago—in Gwen's blood. He turned to the next girl's photo.

"Now that one's interesting. She was a Miss America finalist before she moved to Vegas and started waiting tables. Left work one night and never showed up at her apartment. Her car disappeared, just like the others. I swear, one day we're going to find a garage full of them."

"You need to search Hawk's property. The house, the grounds. There's evidence there."

"Like I said, be *patient*." He cocked one brow at Dario. "We've got to see where he leads us. Just give us a few days. We need just a little more if we're going to put him away and actually keep him there."

Dario lowered his head to his hands and squeezed his temples. He thought back.

Meeting Hawk and Gwen in Biloxi.

The date with Gwen, the night when Jenny killed herself, where Gwen's eyes had darted to the exits, and she seemed positively terrified.

Hawk's job offer. Gwen's confession, her plea, her need to be rescued.

He'd always been a sucker for a damsel in distress. She had needed someone, and he had all but tripped over himself to save her from her father.

But he hadn't, had he? In the end, despite their thirteen years together, despite all of his promises, he'd failed her. Even worse, he'd sparked the event that had led to her death.

Dario sat back with a frustrated exhale. "If the recording isn't enough to keep him locked up on Gwen's death, then arrest him on something else. Fuck, he's bribed half of the city. Don't you have anything on that? Or on tax evasion? Or..."

His mind grasped wildly, trying to find something, some way that—in all the time he'd known the man—he had slipped up. But Robert Hawk was smart. He paid the right people. Covered his tracks well and was always just on the right side of legitimate, always a little more interested in money over violence.

Money. The word stuck in his mind, and he mulled over it, lifting his head to see the detective shake a sugar packet into his coffee mug and sloshing the contents around. "With Gwen deceased, do you have the authority to access her financials?"

The man hesitated, the coffee cup almost to his lips, then nodded. "Sure. With her death being a murder, we can look through her financials to research her life, try and find someone with a motive." He fixed his eyes on Dario. "Though, I gotta say, financially speaking, there's not a better person than you, in terms of profiting from her death."

Dario said nothing, his focus shifting through the accounts that Gwen had access to. "She's on some of Hawk's private accounts. Use that access to dig up anything you can. And the business accounts as well. Bribes, tax evasion, there's got to be something in those accounts."

"You realize that Gwen's on *your* accounts, too. Opening this can of worms ... it may come back to bite you."

Dario shrugged off the threat. At this point, a bite was the least of his worries. They needed to drown Robert Hawk. Cut him off at the knees, handcuff him for every crime he'd ever committed, and hold him accountable for the monster he was.

And the sooner all of that happened, the sooner Bell would be safe.

SEVEN

ROBERT HAWK

Two decades ago, Robert Hawk had sat at his desk and watched a grainy handheld video where monsters damaged his child. The memory of it had never left him. It was one of the reasons he never sexually touched his pets, and a large part of the reason that he had always, once Gwen returned from Mexico, kept close tabs on her.

Leaving her in Mexico had been a calculated decision. You pay kidnappers once, and you'll have a kidnapping problem forever. He had done the right thing, though Gwen had never seemed to appreciate the sacrifice. Of course, there had been a risk to her life. He'd known that then, and balanced out that risk with the knowledge that he had, should the situation turn badly, a second child.

Now, he watched a new video, one of his second daughter running down the interior hall of the house. She exited out the back door without looking back. He rewound the footage and re-watched it. Clicked through the other camera feeds and found nothing. She had been smart. Hidden in the pockets and covered her tracks.

He closed the video and let out a hard sigh, swiveling in his chair and looking out the window at the view.

He had learned about Claudia two months before her birth. The pregnant piece of trash who had shown up at the casino hadn't been thinking when she had blabbed the news to his secretary in a thinly veiled threat. And the timing, which coincided with Gwen's mother's illness... had been inconvenient.

But Robert Hawk always paid his debts, and he paid the pregnant slut's—sending an attorney over with a hefty check and an ironclad agreement that insured that the bitch would keep her mouth shut and never share the paternity with anyone, including the child.

He'd hoped for a boy and been incensed by the news of another girl. Disappointments, they all were. Dario had been the closest thing he'd had to a son, and even he—in the end—had failed.

But that was another issue that would be solved on another day. For now, he had to decide what to do with Claudia.

In her continual and desperate quest for his approval, he had seen the pride shining in her eyes, the exuberance she'd shown when she believed she had killed little Bell Hartley.

But she hadn't. She'd made a *mistake*. And in his world, mistakes carried deadly consequences, ones that Dario Capece and Bell Hartley would soon realize.

But first, Claudia needed to be dealt with. To forgive or to punish?

One option would leave him with a daughter. The other would allow Claudia to finally meet her sister, in death.

BELL

Everything was different in this place. I sat on the couch, my feet tucked underneath me, and half-heartedly watched a local real estate show. It was terrible. All of the women were either wearing way too much makeup, or hadn't even bothered to brush their hair. One man was in cargo shorts and Crocs, another wore a suit and seemed fresh off the timeshare sales circuit. But still, it was better than the news.

Everything seemed muted. Even the heat seemed to leave me alone, the doors of the house open, sweat sticking the shirt to Laurent's back. I watched television, stared out the window, and thought about Gwen.

The guilt was different from when I was raped. I realized now, as an adult, and with a realistic understanding of the situation, that I wasn't at fault. This was a different beast entirely. The effects of my actions hadn't been my parents fighting, or a police officer's ridicule. A woman had died. A woman who, from every news report, had been an angel. Loved by everyone. Philanthropic. Kind. Genuine. Beautiful.

I had watched a dozen specials, all filled with glowing accounts of a woman who seemed to dwarf me in every category. I had watched a slideshow of images of her and Dario. Gwen, in a beaded wedding gown, in a ceremony that rivaled a royal wedding. Dario, gazing at her with adoration. The two of them, in glitz and glamour, at charity events, with celebrities, and at exotic locations. The photos had filled me with a mixture of jealousy and despair, my knowledge of their 'relationship' in sharp contrast to every photo I saw.

They looked like the perfect couple. Madly in love. Two puzzle pieces that fit. I had always been in awe of Dario's magnitude and presence. Gwen seemed to have that same brilliance, a gem that could hold her own when placed beside him.

And me? I sank into a couch that smelled slightly of Febreze and thought of my 2.7 GPA. My job at The House. I'd thought that I was doing so well. My own place, though it had been packed with three other women. My blossoming bank account, which was approaching ten thousand dollars. My foolish pride in things that, compared to Gwen, were pathetic.

My guilt worsened, my jealousy against a dead woman, who had died in my place, was evidence of exactly how shallow and insecure I was.

It was too much to take. The guilt. The insecurity. The jealousy. I curled into the arm of the couch and stared at the screen and wished I had gotten to the suite just a little bit earlier. If I had, Gwen would still be alive. *And I would have died.* And Vegas would have moved on with little to no ripple effect.

I watched as a man gestured to a marsh view, and listened as Laurent stomped through the house, the lamp beside me trembling from his heavy steps. I closed my eyes, hoping he wouldn't talk to me, and thought about Gwen.

Night fell on day two. In the carport, seven men crowded around the table, their elbows bumping, beers littering the surface. They were playing a card game I'd never heard of. I'd started out there, eavesdropping on them while I pretended to clean my tennis shoe, but I couldn't figure out the rules of the game and finally headed back in.

"Hey Bell!" Laurent shouted at me, and I tilted my head far enough left to see him. I raised my eyebrows, and he waved at me. "Joe is out, we need you to play."

I stood up and trudged through the kitchen, stopping in the doorway and crossing my arms over my chest. "I don't know how to play."

"That's okay." He nodded to the chair beside him, a scrawny man easing out of it and moving around the table, a dour look on his face. Probably Joe, the loser. Looking at the puny chip stack he cradled, Laurent would probably be next. He patted the seat. "Sit. Just eye us for a bit."

I squeezed around the edge of the table and caught a few glances from the men around the table. They all looked like the sort that spent their days doing manual labor, their clothes faded, beards long, faces tan. A couple of them smiled in greeting, but most looked down at their cards as if they contained nuclear launch codes.

I sat down next to Laurent, who grabbed the bottom of my folding chair and dragged it across the concrete until it was flush with his. He lifted up the edge of his hand and showed me the five cards.

I glanced over them, the values meaning nothing to me. From inside, my phone rang, and I straightened at the sound of it. I suffered two bumped knees and a stubbed toe by the time I made it to the living room. Grabbing my phone from the couch, I caught a glimpse of a Vegas number and answered it.

"Hey." Dario sounded exhausted, the simple word coated in weight and dragging along the bottom of the phone line.

"Hey." The word came out a little too breathless, something I blamed entirely on my sprint through the house, and not due to my heart, which was presently soaring through my ribcage. *I'd missed him.* His voice, his strength, his reassurance, and his kiss.

Dario stole the words from me, his voice gruff. "I've missed you."

I blinked back tears. "Are you okay? I saw on the news that you were arrested."

He sighed. "I'm fine. Don't believe everything you see on the news. I'm doing my best to get this psychopath behind bars."

"Did you?"

"Not yet." He cleared his throat. "Where are you?"

I glanced back at the carport, and moved farther away from the group, opening the front door and easing out of it. "Same place I've been for two days. Laurent's house. There are a bunch of his friends over, playing some card game."

"Bourré, probably." He pronounced it "boo-ray," and I recognized the name.

"Yeah, that's it." I pulled the door shut and stepped onto the small front porch, one covered in a healthy layer of dirt. "I thought you couldn't make phone calls from jail."

His voice dropped a little, and I strained to hear the background on his call. "I'm not exactly a prisoner. The arrest was a show, one to lull Gwen's father into a false sense of security. We're hoping he'll make a mistake. In the meantime, I've been handed over to the feds and out of the hands of the local cops—half of who are on Hawk's payroll."

My anxiety about his situation rose, and I felt helplessly out of touch. I leaned against the porch post and stared out into the woods.

"Any of Laurent's friends hit on you?" The protective jealousy in his voice was so adolescent, so utterly normal, that I laughed, a bit of my tension releasing.

"No. Honestly, they seem a little afraid of me."

"Good. I know every one of those assholes. They better be." His voice changed, softening. "I called your parents."

"You did?" I straightened, hating the fact that I couldn't call them myself and let them know I was okay.

"Yes. I let them know you were safe and that you'd call them soon. I need you to last a few more days, Bell. No phone calls. No contact with anyone."

I nodded, forgetting that he couldn't see me, tears pricking at the edges of my eyes. He sounded so strong, so in control, so calm. It was such a different picture than the man who had fallen apart over Gwen's body, his emotions fraying, composure gone. "How were they? Did they sound okay?"

"They were fine. And I have men next door, and they've created a security perimeter of cameras and motion sensors around their home. They're safe."

They're safe. It was meant to be a reassuring comment, but did the exact opposite. My chest tightened, a wave of nausea moving through me, and I found my way to the step and sat down. I hadn't even *thought* about my parent's safety, the possibility of Hawk finding and hurting them in an effort to get to me. They were at risk, and all because I couldn't keep my hands to myself and my heart focused on a normal guy. I should have ignored my lack of feelings and kept seeing Ian. He had been safe. No wife. No empire. No crazy father-in-law who may or may not torture cocktail waitresses on the weekend.

But Ian... Ian had never had a chance, not against the hold that Dario had had on me, from the very beginning. And that reality had brought on all of this. Gwen's death. My own risk. And now... my parents were in danger. Were Rick and Lance, also? What about Meredith? My roommates?

I tried to breathe, worked to find something to focus on. I remembered an exercise my school therapist had taught me after my rape and attempted to find five things to see.

My shoe, still stained from the dirt. *One.*

A wet leaf, stuck to the porch. *Two.*

The row of trucks, on the edge of the house. *Three.*

Laurent's boots, stacked by the door. *Four.*

My hand, trembling on my jeans. *Five.*

I tucked my fingers into a fist and held it against my stomach. I thought about my dad, and how slowly he climbed the front steps into the house. His awkward stretch to reach the hunting rifle he has hanging over the back door. I pinched my eyes closed and struggled to return to the exercise. *Five things to see.*

Four things you can touch.

I uncoiled my fist and reached out, running a hand over the damp wood on the porch, the surface bumpy, the paint more worn off than present. *One.*

"Bell?"

I ignored him and propped the phone against my shoulder, moving a hand to the knee of my sweatpants, ones I washed and dried this morning. The material was thick and soft, and I rubbed my fingertips along the cheap side seam. *Two.*

I placed my hand on my neck, pulling the neck of my T-shirt down and putting my hand over my heart, the skin warm, my heartbeat quick. I took a deep breath and exhaled. *Three.*

"Bell!"

"Just a minute." I mumbled the words and looked over the porch, not wanting to stand, finding a twig that had fallen on the bottom step, a few feet away. I strained forward to reach it, and closed my hand around it, the strong stick reassuring in my grip. *Four. Four things to touch.*

Three things you can hear. I closed my eyes. Focused on the soft sounds from inside, the low murmur of voices.

Someone laughed.

A car door quietly shut.

Crickets, loud and persistent, buzzed.

The constant sounds were relaxing, and I rested my head against the post, my hand tightening and loosening on the stick, and focused on the chirp of the crickets for several long seconds. *Three things you can hear.*

Two things you can smell. Lime. There was a faint scent of it in the air, and I remembered watching Laurent spread a line of it along the perimeter of the yard to keep snakes away.

I blocked out the scent and tried to find another, something more than the humid blanket that defines this place. *There.* A wisp of something. Something familiar. Expensive. Refined. Wild. Something that smelled of power and sexuality. Something that had made me swoon and buckle and yield and fall in love.

I snapped my eyes open and saw him there. I didn't move, didn't breathe, didn't do anything to disrupt the moment, certain that it was a mirage, my panic creating something that didn't exist.

He crouched before me, his eyes tender, and reached forward, cupping my neck, his thumb gently tracing along my skin. "It's okay."

I dropped the stick and grabbed his shirt. My cell hit the porch, and I clawed up his chest, staring at him. "How are you—?"

He pressed his lips to my forehead, then my cheek, sitting down on the step and pulling me into his lap. I curled against his chest like a child and a sob broke from my chest. Tears ran down my cheeks and his arms wrapped around me, hugging me tightly, his body warm and powerful.

"It's okay. It's okay—" His voice cracked, and he pulled away enough to see my face. The guilt in his eyes, the weight of it on his handsome features ... it broke my heart. I tried to smile, and his face only grew more concerned. "I'm so sorry, Bell. I'm so sorry."

I sat up, closer to him, and felt his hands tighten. I gripped the back of his neck and pulled his mouth to mine. Our kiss crashed like a kite into a storm. A battle of lips and tongue, need and sorrow. His hand twisted in my hair, pulled me tighter, and our mouths became a frantic mess of small quick contact, and deeper, rough tastes. He broke away and whispered *I love you* in the moment before he reclaimed my mouth. He dominated and healed, reassured me and begged. In that kiss, a part of us broke apart and then fused back together.

Two things to smell. *One thing to taste.*

EIGHT

He lifted me off the step, his mouth frantic, stealing kisses as if worried I'd disappear. He got me on my feet and walked me backward, his arm around my body, keeping me close to his chest. He fumbled with the door, got it open, and kept his mouth on me as we made our way into the living room. He didn't hesitate, pushing me toward Laurent's bedroom.

"Hey D."

The guy on the couch mumbled the greeting and Dario ignored him, nipping at my bottom lip before devouring my neck, his hands feverishly working under the hem of my sweatshirt and dipping under the waist of the pants. I leaned my head back, closing my eyes at the feel of his tongue against my neck, a delicious combination of suction and aggression that had my body twitching in anticipation.

In three steps we were through the door to Laurent's room and he was kicking the door shut and pushing me toward the bed, his eyes dark with arousal. "I need you so fucking bad."

I ripped off the sweatshirt, and he hooked his fingers in my sweatpants and worked them over my hips. I reached for his jeans, and he straightened, watching as I parted his fly and dragged down the zipper. I stared at the hard outline of his cock, hanging to the right side, and ran my fingers over the cotton, then gripped him through the fabric.

"Come on, Bell. Touch it."

I pulled the black fabric down, exposing the top of his shaft, thin veins bulging, his olive skin tight. I glanced up at him. His eyes were dark with need, his features pinched, gaze tight on me. I pulled the fabric lower, till his cock broke free and bobbed out. When I gripped it, he groaned. The beautiful organ was swollen, the head glistening with a drop of precum. I leaned forward and captured the drop with my tongue, an action that caused his thighs to twitch under my palms, his legs parting a little to give me better access.

"Suck it. Please."

I heard a rumble of voices from the carport and ignored them, my knees hitting the carpet, my hand fisting his thick shaft. I lowered my head and began to work my lips over his head, my tongue against the underside, my cheeks hollowing as I increased the suction.

He hissed, his fingers tightening on my hair and he enjoyed the sensation for several minutes before pulling me off and nodding to the bed. "Get on your knees. Bent over."

I scrambled back, turning around, finding my way across the dark surface, dimly lit by the moonlight coming in the window. My elbows hit the mattress, ass in the air.

He left my panties on and ran a hand over the curve of my butt, sliding a hand under the cotton and taking a leisurely tour over my ass cheeks. I peeked back and saw his cock jutting out, the thick head of it swinging through the air between his muscular thighs. His grip tightened. "Fuck, I missed you."

I felt his fingers slide along the edge of my panties, pushing the fabric into my crack, my ass cheeks exposed, his touch roaming over their bare surface.

"I've needed you." His hand slid down, talented fingers playing over my damp opening, moves that had my back arching, a moan slipping out. He kept me on my knees, but yanked at the cotton of my panties, pulling them over my ass and down my legs, and I was naked.

I swallowed. "I'm so glad you are here."

His forefingers pushed in between my folds, just an inch of penetration, and my composure buckled. I gasped out his name and he leaned forward, running his hand up my stomach and cupping my bare breasts, squeezing them as he worked his fingers in and out of me.

"Roll over for me."

I obeyed, loose and needy, my legs tumbling over his arms as he continued the casual manipulation of my most sensitive area. He ripped open a condom package and worked it on as I tightened around his finger, my orgasm building, my G-spot swelling, and fell flat on my back. He lifted one of my ankles to his shoulder, watched my face as the orgasm approached, then delicately delivered the sweetest pleasure in the world.

My back arched, my hands clawed in an attempt to reach him, and he rolled a wet digit over my clit as he fucked me with his fingers, the orgasm blindingly sharp. Waves of intensity hit, my cries growing louder, and the angles changed as he crawled on top and silenced me with his mouth.

God, I've missed his kiss. The domination of it, the surrender of everything as I yielded to the strong sweeps of his tongue, the give and take of his power, the raw energy that fueled my arousal and built everything to a higher degree. When we kissed, I felt more alive, more vulnerable, more protected, more afraid. I kissed him and was terrified I would never feel this way again. I kissed him and—

He pulled his fingers from me and I whimpered, needing more, the orgasm not yet done. I clawed at his shoulders, and then he thrusted forward, his cock pushing in, and I was whole.

Better than whole. He drove deeper, his cock almost painful in its girth, and I fell apart, the orgasm sinking, tremors of pleasure quaking as it disappeared and a guttural need to be dominated took its place.

"Harder." I grunted the word, my nails digging into his back, my mouth took again by his kiss, this time rougher, our teeth hitting, tongues colliding, breaths panting as he rocked his hips back and slammed forward, the depth causing a sharp pain. He groaned and I swore, crying out for more.

In between the blur of his thrusts, the waves of the pleasure, the intensity of the expanding energy ... I saw glimpses of him. His abs tensed. A bicep braced. His eyes, tight on the place where our bodies met. His cock, slick and stiff, sliding out of me, then back inside.

It was raw. It was primal. It was a punishment and a salve, all at once. I took his furious motions and needed every thrust of it.

I rolled over, sticky from his come, and rested my head on his chest.

His hand settled on my head. "I love you."

"I love you too." I closed my eyes, my limbs cooperating as he hauled me higher on his body, my legs intertwined with his, our torsos now stacked on top of each other.

"I'm so sorry, Bell." His voice cracked, and I lifted my head until I could see the misery on his face. It was a look that broke my heart.

I crawled higher up his chest until our faces were level, and I kissed his cheek, his forehead, his nose. "Don't apologize."

"Just let me. I can't—" He sighed. "I can't say it to Gwen, let me at least say it to you."

I paused above his mouth, then slowly lowered my lips to his and kissed them softly. When I pulled off, he met my eyes for one of the first times all night.

"I forgive you," I whispered.

It was a stupid thing to say. I was as much to blame for this as he was. We had both been selfish, and she had been the one to suffer for our sins. Still, the words seemed to do something to him. His face cleared, the pain a little less etched in those strong features. He pulled me closer, and I lay atop his body, my hand over his heart, comforted by the heavy thud of the organ.

I closed my eyes and wanted to stay in the moment forever.

I woke up as I was moved. My legs lifted and manipulated. A hand gripped my waist. I tried to sit up and my knee jabbed into something that cursed.

"Ouch."

"What's going on?" I allowed myself to be pulled upright.

Dario worked the sweatpants back over my hips. "I can't find your panties."

My eyes adjusted to the dim light and I pointed out the pair, then helped him with my shirt and sweatshirt, the sleep daze evaporating. "Are we going somewhere?"

He sat down on the bed beside me. "I've got to get back to Vegas. I could only skip out on jail for the one night."

He kissed me on the forehead and it became abundantly clear that this was it, he was about to leave, and I'd be alone with my thoughts again.

I pulled on his hand. "Take me with you."

He shook his head. "I can't. It's not safe for you, in Vegas."

I followed him to the door, my anxiety growing. "Can't you just surround me with guards and lock me away somewhere?"

He stopped and turned to face me. "I don't trust my guys. I don't trust *anyone* right now except for this group."

He jabbed a finger in the direction of the poker game, which had fallen silent. "I know you're safe here. And that's the only thing keeping me sane right now."

I frowned, and he pulled me to him. "It won't be much longer, I promise. We're closing in on Gwen's father. I have a plan."

"It was definitely her father?" I was afraid to ask if he was wrong. Afraid to think about the fact that there might be someone *else* out there that might want me—or Gwen—dead.

His face tightened. "Yes." His voice grew strained. "He all but admitted it to me, before he found out he had Gwen killed by accident." He leaned forward and kissed me, a quick hard brush of lips that didn't ease my panic.

I reluctantly let go as he moved away. "I..." I wanted to say so many things. I wanted to thank him for coming. I wanted to tell him that I would be fine without him, even though it felt like a lie. I watched him lace up his shoes and ached at the pain that lined his face. He had so much on him right now. Gwen's death. My safety. I straightened my shoulders and fought to keep the weakness out of my voice. "I don't want you to worry about me." I moved off the bed. "I'm fine here. Bored stiff. I feel guilty. But..." my voice warbled slightly. "I'm fine. Just focus on your stuff."

He stood and stepped forward, meeting me in the middle of the dark room. The bathroom lamp lit his features, and I could see the way his gaze searched mine. "I hate abandoning you out here, but it's for your own—"

I stopped him with a kiss. "I know. And I'm fine. I just wish..." Emotions welled and I struggled to tamper them down. "I'm so sorry," I whispered. "About her."

His mouth crumbled a little, the edge of his lips breaking before he pinned them together and brusquely nodded. "It wasn't us, Bell. Her father... he did this. Not us. Don't let yourself take on that burden."

I nodded tightly, and his face softened.

"It's hard for me, because I imagine, if it had been you, how differently I would feel. And that makes me feel as if I'm disrespecting her—" He broke off the sentence with a swear. "It's just hell, what you and I are in right now. But, I love you. Miss you."

He pulled me forward and planted a soft kiss on my forehead. "I'll see you soon."

He opened the bedroom door, gave me one final look, and walked out.

NINE

I laid in Laurent's bed and listened to an engine start, heard the squeal of a belt as it reversed, then left. I rolled onto one side and thought about this disaster. It was like that puzzle that we worked on together, a pile of undone pieces that had to be sorted through and put into place. Only ... it felt as if a timer was running, a countdown of sorts, Dario's hands furiously picking through pieces and snapping them into place, and not quick enough to beat the clock.

What would happen when it hit zero, and the puzzle was incomplete? Would Hawk go free? Would he find and kill me?

I listened as the engine rumble grew softer, and had the sudden, panicked urge to sprint out the front door and chase him down. I got up and found my phone. Scrolled through to the number that Dario had called me from last night. I hit the green phone icon, and it connected.

"Hey."

I crawled back into bed and pulled the covers over me, curling into a ball on my side. "Hey."

"I'll have to ditch this phone when I get on the plane."

The thought of him being unreachable, of more days of silence and unknowing... I crushed my feelings into a tiny ball and swallowed them, trying to find some inner strength. "How long do you think it'll take for them to arrest Gwen's dad?"

He sighed, and there was the sound of wind in the background, static on the line. "I'm battling with the feds over what they're doing now—which is trying to lure him into leading us to the professional who killed her—or finding something minor to arrest him for. Then, once he's in custody, they're hoping to search his homes and find something that's gonna lock him away forever."

"So, a hit man?" The words sounded cartoonish when coming from my lips. "He hired someone like that?"

"That's my best guess. He would never have mistaken Gwen for you. And he wouldn't have shot from behind. He would have wanted to confront you before pulling the trigger. He would have wanted you to know exactly why he was doing it. That's just the sort of man he is."

He spoke about it so matter-of-factly, and it was almost enough to insulate the impact of the words, of the real-life situation that almost occurred. I rolled onto my back and stared up at the dark blades of Laurent's ceiling fan. I searched for a new topic. "You said they might arrest him for something minor. Like what?"

"White collar crimes. We haven't exactly dotted every i in the last ten years. I've given the FBI access to our financials, plus they can dig through anything with Gwen's name on it. Their forensic accountants should find plenty to work with."

"But that would implicate you, also. Right?"

"Yes. They've agreed to grant me some immunity, and are going to first focus on the bank accounts that he and Gwen shared. But there's a risk I will be charged as well. Legitimately charged—not the fake arrest. I didn't—"

His voice broke off, and I filled in the gap. *I didn't kill Gwen.*

"I know you didn't." It seemed like an important statement to make. And I believed it.

"I've got to go." He paused, and the next words came out haltingly. "I love you."

"I love you too," I whispered the words, and they felt as flimsy as tissue.

Did our love, at that point, even matter? Had it all been for nothing given that our world, our future, had been obliterated? The feds were digging into Hawk, and from that research, Dario might be arrested. He might go to jail. He'd lost his best friend. His empire had lost their matriarch. Would Dario eventually associate loving me with this tragedy? Would he resent me for it?

I rolled onto one side and hugged one of Laurent's pillows. I wanted to be on my parents' couch watching television with Dad while I worked on schoolwork. I wanted my mom to come sit with me and brush my hair like she did when I was a kid. I wanted her hugs, and the assurances that everything was going to be okay. I gripped the pillow tighter and fought the loneliness, the desperate urge to call them.

LAS VEGAS PD

At 2 am, a meeting was held between the feds and the police chief. In the day since Dario Capece's 'arrest', Robert Hawk hadn't led them anywhere. There had been no suspicious calls, and no leads to whom he had hired for the hit. The FBI was getting itchy, and their forensic accounting team had uncovered enough bribery and mail fraud evidence to build a solid case. A terse discussion was had, dicks were pulled out and measured, and then a decision was made.

At 4 am, the team sat quietly, their backs against the walls of the vehicle, and listened to their captain. The cramped compartment smelled faintly of body odor, and the van bounced over a pothole, jostling them in their places.

Captain Dowdey finished his orders as the van came to a stop before the Vegas mansion. Gripping the paperwork firmly in one hand, he said a silent prayer and stepped out of the vehicle.

Sometimes it was easy. Sometimes you knocked on a door, and they opened it up and smiled at you—a smile that deflated when the arrest warrant was flashed, their shoulders sagging, body obediently turning to allow you to snap on the cuffs.

Most of the time, it wasn't easy. Assholes crawled out windows and ran. Sometimes a mentally-unhinged individual locked himself in a back bedroom with an automatic rifle, intent on killing as many uniforms as possible before going down.

Captain Dowdey climbed up the front steps and rapped on the door. Behind him, his men lifted their muzzles in preparation. As he waited, he hoped that this would be one of the easy ones.

After a moment, the man himself opened the door, dressed to impress, despite the early hour. He stepped forward and the dawn light illuminated his suit, one that must have put him back at least ten grand.

Dowdey shifted in his cheap pants, his Danner boots creaking in protest, and put on his best smile. "Mr. Hawk, I apologize for the early visit, but we are here to place you under arrest."

"Ah." Hawk adjusted the line of his suit. "And what, may I ask, are you arresting me for?"

"Bribery of a public official. Eight counts." He resisted the urge to extend the arrest warrant, the gesture too similar to that of a child showing off a shiny toy.

"Bribery?" The man widened his eyes theatrically. "Now, that's a federal crime. But you..." He waved a finger in the direction of the man. "You're a local badge. And, what is your name?"

From behind the captain, Agent King stepped forward. "Don't you worry, Mr. Hawk. We're here too."

The captain spoke up. "And I'm Captain Dowdey."

The older man smiled, a gesture void of threat, as if they were two men waiting in line, discussing sports stats. "Ah yes. *James* Dowdey, right? You've got that lovely new bride..." His voice dropped off as he tucked his hands into his pocket and looked up at the ceiling, his face scrunching in thought. "Jennifer. James and Jennifer. Cute. Congratulations. There's nothing more valuable to a man than his family."

The friendly smile didn't slip; the threat easily missed if one wasn't looking for it. They'd found the bribery records in the bank statements. The intimidation ... the coercion... that had been harder to prove in the last twenty-four hours. It was there; it was just impossible to get any officer to admit to it. As Hawk so clearly pointed out, there was little more valuable to a man than his family.

The Captain cleared his throat and stepped forward, keeping an eye on the two armed men who stood behind Hawk. They didn't move, their hands still and visible, and he nodded to them as he pulled on Hawk's shoulder, turning him away and grabbing one wrist as delicately as he could manage. The urge to wrench his arm from his socket, to painfully twist the joint and get the old man down on one knee ... he let out a slow breath and focused on pulling his cuffs out and snapping one on.

He began to recite the Miranda rights.

THE CRAZY

In the bookstore, they had thought she was crazy. Funny how they were the ones who were actually chained up. Maybe not in a concrete cell, like she had been, but metaphorically speaking, they were chained by their jobs, their debts. Their dogged pursuits of money and material things. They didn't understand, *couldn't* understand the base principals that guided them.

She understood. That sort of clarity was realized when everything was taken away from you. When your life disappears, you realize the stupid things about it that you missed. Those stupid things showed your weaknesses. Robert had exposed all of hers. Shown her the triviality of them all. Released her from her shackles and given her a new life. A new purpose.

She'd gone back once. He'd opened the door to the warehouse and placed the car key in her hand. Told her to return to her old life and see what she had missed.

His timing, as always, had been impeccable. It had been Christmas day. She'd walked into her mother's house and seen the signs everywhere. Materialism, dripping from the gift boxes and shopping bags. Gluttony, in the full table, sugary desserts and fat-ladened dishes. Insecurity, always present, her mother's latest boyfriend as weak and uninteresting as all the others had been.

There had been lots of hugs. Tears. Words that meant nothing from a woman who had taught her nothing, *nothing* her entire life.

"Are you okay?" A stranger touched her arm and she snapped back to the present.

"I'm fine." She stepped away, bumping into a woman, the downtown street crowded, people everywhere. Rats, that's what they all were. Rats in mazes. Running around oblivious to their lack of purpose.

She spied a crosswalk and walked toward it, her eyes skipping over the buildings, looking for a place to hunker down for a few hours and hide. An electronics store caught her eye, the front display full of television screens, a name jumping out at her from the ticker on the bottom.

HAWK arrested. It was just a fleeting moment, the font whizzing by, replaced by useless sports updates and a hurricane warning somewhere in Florida. She stayed in place, her nose to the glass, waiting for the reel to return, and when it finally did, she inhaled sharply at what it said.

ON CHARGES OF BRIBERY, CASINO MOGUL ROBERT HAWK HAS BEEN ARRESTED.

Fucking rats.

BELL

"Come ya."

Something poked at my calf and the sheet, which was tangled around me, tugged.

"Get up. Day's a wasting."

I rolled over and blinked at Laurent, taking in the plaid shirt and khakis—an interesting departure from his standard attire of fishing shirts and jeans. "Why are *you* all dressed up?"

He smacked my leg and nodded to the bathroom. "*Allons.* We running out of time."

I sat up slowly, rubbing a sore spot on the side of my neck. "Running out of time for what?"

"Church. It's Sunday, lazy bones."

Church. The concept was so unexpected that I dropped my hand from my neck and turned to him. "Church? You're going to church?"

He shook his head, his large hands coming to rest on his hips. "No, not me. We. Now go on and get washed up. We leaving in fifteen minutes."

I didn't move. "You want *me* to go to church?"

He grinned, his face creasing around the gesture. "Don't worry, chere. You won't catch fire."

Catching fire hadn't exactly been my concern. I slowly stood, grateful that Dario had had the sense to dress me before leaving. "Why do I have to come? Can't I just stay here?"

From behind me, the bed beckoned. It'd be so easy to turn back around, crawl into the sheets, and go back to sleep. And during sleep, I didn't have to think about Gwen, or Hawk, or anything. I started to get back on the bed, and Laurent caught my waist with a hand the size of a baseball glove.

"Ah, ah, ah. You going to church, because I'm not leaving you here. Boss man's orders."

I groaned, and any warm and fuzzies that may have accumulated during Dario's pillow talk last night, vanished. "I don't really go to church."

He chuckled. "You don't say. The little thing with the married man?" He wagged a finger at me as if I was a child. "Maybe you should. Be a lot less of a mess you in."

I glared at him. "That sentence doesn't even make sense."

He clapped his hands, and the unexpected crack caused me to jump. "Now! Git or I be bringing Septime in here."

I got. I could hear the shift of the living room floor as she moved and could imagine her striding in here, shoving me into the bathroom, and stripping me like a disobedient toddler.

I delicately trudged into the bathroom and turned on the shower, the red and orange number, hanging on a hook off the wall, caught my eye. I carefully lifted it, eyeing the dress, a size small, a clear indicator that it was for me.

"There's a dress for you, hanging on the hook."

"I found it." I held it up against me, grimacing at the length, which ended right around my calves. It looked like the sort of thing an Amish wife would wear—if she liked gaudy colors and lace-trimmed collars. "Where did you get this?"

"It was my Momma's."

Great. Good thing I hadn't insulted it. I gingerly hung it back on the hook and tried to imagine a size small woman who had birthed both Laurent and Septime. Poor thing. I hope they had the good drugs back then. A natural birth ... I shuddered at the thought.

A fist pounded on the door and I glared in the direction of it.

"Be patient!"

"We leaving in ten minutes. If I need to, I'll send Septime in after ya."

Ten minutes. Ten minutes to shower and put on a dress that would make me the laughing stock of church.

Church. A place I hadn't been in a dozen years. A place I probably didn't belong within ten miles of.

I pulled off the sweatshirt and cursed Dario's name to hell.

TEN

ROBERT HAWK

Some men, like some women, were designed for cages. They had the mentality that needed the rules and structure, yearned for the simple rewards of food and silence.

He was not that man, and the fact that he was in handcuffs right now was unacceptable. Especially given all of the money he paid to this department. Over a million dollars, last year alone, in discreet white envelopes, cash changing hands as regularly as whore abortions. A million dollars and he was in the back of this disgusting car, on a seat frequented by drug users and losers.

He shifted against the vinyl and contained his temper, swallowing all that he wanted to say. He watched the city move past, still wakening, the tourists not yet out, the worker bees in motion, and clenched his jaw shut.

Some men were designed for cages. He was designed to be the one who put them there, who punished the weak and disciplined their sins.

Gwen's death was Dario's sin. Had he not bedded that skank, brought her to The Majestic, flaunted her under Gwen's nose—Hawk wouldn't have had to act. He wouldn't have needed to involve Claudia. And Gwen ... Gwen wouldn't have even been there, no doubt trying to understand Dario's deceit, trying to save her marriage, trying to—

He bit the inside of his cheek so hard that he tasted blood. A waste, that's what it all was. A waste of bending over backward to give Gwen everything. A waste of training and testing Claudia, only to have her fail in the most unforgivable of ways. A waste of investing time and energy into Dario, a man who had stabbed him in the back after all that he had given him.

He'd kill them all, starting with Bell Hartley. Then Dario. And then, after she'd had a few weeks to crawl back to him on her weak little belly, he'd kill Claudia too.

It was necessary. A cleansing of the scum. And then, with all of them gone, he'd come out of retirement and take his empire back. He wasn't too old to rule. To inspire. To control.

The police car turned into the station and his shoulders tightened at the crowd that filled the parking lot, a mix of cameras, uniforms, and gawkers, despite the early hour. He couldn't get a goddamn reporter to cover a bacteria rumor at a competitor's restaurant, but they could all be guaranteed to show up here, flashbulbs blazing, for this ridiculous circus of an arrest. Bullshit, that's what it was. Absolute bullshit. A million dollars in bribes to this department and he was dealing with this bullshit.

"Tell me you aren't going to walk me through that crowd."

The man behind the wheel nodded. "We'll get you inside as quickly as we can."

This was intentional, all of it. They were *punishing* him, and he couldn't understand why. He'd just lost his daughter for Christ's sake. Couldn't they give him some respect and time to mourn? For them to arrest him now, for *bribery* of all things... it reeked of interference. Someone was behind all of this, pulling strings.

He'd find that individual and wrap those strings around their neck.

The car door opened, and the sound of the crowd, of questions and shutters, the crunch of steps against gravel—all of it hit Robert Hawk at once. He lifted one Ferragamo shoe out, watching the glossy shine of the leather. Setting it down, he struggled to step out of the car without the use of his arms, the cuffs biting painfully into his wrists as he fought. No one could do this. It didn't have anything to do with his age. It was a geometry problem that didn't have a solution. The center of gravity was too far off, and now—as another insult—the officer would have to help him out of the car.

He shouldered off the first uniform, heaving his way from the low car and swaying slightly as he found his footing and straightened. His right elbow was grabbed by the second uniform and pulled forward, toward the crowd, a small path now visible through them and up to the building's front steps.

Just a day ago, he'd watched with smug glee as Dario had been led through a similar group and to those same doors. He'd crowed with satisfaction and enjoyed the haunted look on Dario's face, the hunch of his big shoulders as he wore the cuffs, the rough calls of the crowd as he'd moved through and to the station.

Just a day ago, and now he walked the same path, was treated the same way, heard the same taunting calls.

"Murderer!"

The deep voice was so strong that it carried above the others, a few stopping in their chants to look over their shoulder, the crowd disturbing a bit, bodies moving, shifting, making way for someone from the back. Hawk paused, his head slowly turning as he looked over the crowd, searching for the source of the accusation.

While Dario had avoided the cameras and slurs like a pussy, he would confront. He was Robert *Hawk*. He—not Dario—owned this town. This arrest would be sorted out, he would be released and order would be restored. He saw the owner of the deep voice. It was paired with a dingy white T-shirt stretched over big shoulders and the lumber of a stride that easily shoved through the crowd. The man stood a head over the others, and when he came fully into view, Hawk was unsurprised to see his jeans and cowboy boots.

Who, the *fuck*, was this?

The man moved his right hand, and it was a blur of action, the motion too quick to respond to. He lifted the gun, and Hawk tensed, his legs bending, old muscles working overtime to launch him forward and out of harm's way.

The gun went off.

Screams.

Movement. Shoving, running. Hawk fell forward without hands to catch himself with and met the unforgiving asphalt face first. The thin skin of his cheek shredded and his nose collided with the ground, a crunch of bone sounding.

Another gunshot.

Another. A volley of them, of screams and panic.

A hand gripped at his shoulder, and jerked him over, onto his back. He looked up and into the officer's face.

"I—" He couldn't get the words out. He wheezed, coughed. Stringy moisture blocked his airway. He felt pressure on his chest and glanced down, the officer's hands on him, his forearms flexing as he bore his weight down on the wound.

The son of a bitch had *shot him*. Here, in front of all of these cameras. Robert Hawk, lying on the pavement like a weak old man. His wrists screamed in pain from the weight of the officer, the cuffs pinching them behind his back, and he tried to speak, to order the man off him, but couldn't manage anything.

Is this what dying felt like? He looked up to the sky, and the pain in his chest grew deeper, blurring his vision and turning everything to red.

BELL

Everyone dies. Dad once woke me up in the middle of the night and pulled me into the living room. He made me sit on the floor, by his feet, and listen to his lengthy and disjointed opinion on death, the drunken gist of it summed up in those two simple words. *Everyone dies.*

Everyone. He'd leaned forward and punctuated the word with a stabbed finger toward my nose. *It's a part of life, Bell. We're born. We live. We die.* It was around then that I noticed the glass bowl sitting on the table, the bottom littered with cigarette butts, their ends damp against the slimy bottom and faux treasure chest. It was around then that I asked where Bubba was and realized that *Everyone* was, in this situation, my goldfish. *Everyone dies.* My goldfish had died because Dad needed a place to stick his cigarette butts and Bubba's bowl had looked like the best bet. Gwen had died because I fell in love with the wrong man.

Now, in a hot and sweaty church service inside a clapboard barn, I watched as the pastor stepped away from the pulpit and stopped before the crowd. Of course, his sermon was about death. Just my luck. I tried to run away from something mentally and ended up tripping over it on my exit.

I shouldn't have let Laurent drag me here. This pastor didn't understand my plight. No one was trying to kill him. His most significant concern was probably paying the utility bill on this barn and worrying about that mustard stain on the sleeve of his jacket. I was willing to bet he'd never been in love with a married man, or surrounded by strangers two thousand miles from home, with a swamp man caretaker who was currently giving me the evil eye. I glared back at Laurent and he sighed, cutting his eyes to the front.

Granted, I *did* bring this on myself. I watched as the pastor carefully took the steps down and started to walk down the barn aisle, his voice rising as he moved. I closed my eyes and listened to the man speak about death. His opinion was a little different than my drunken father's had been. His opinion spoke of the forgiveness that we could experience if we simply asked God for his mercy. Dad's soliloquy had been more focused on Bubba's short lifespan, and the fact that he would have been poisoned to death slowly and painfully, had Dad simply dropped the cigarettes in without flushing him down the toilet first.

I felt a sharp elbow in my side and almost yelped. Whipping my head to the right, I gave Septime a dirty look.

"Don't fall asleep." She mouthed the words in an exaggerated fashion that a lip reader three states away would see.

"I'm NOT." I rubbed my side and glowered at her elbows, which should be registered as a weapon. Taking the opportunity to sneak a look at her watch, I wondered how much longer this service could last.

TWO HOURS. Two *hours* is how long we stayed in that barn, the temperature rising as the morning passed. We talked about a lot more than death. There was a giant hugging circle that occurred, where everyone wandered around and hugged and blessed each other. I was introduced a dozen or so times as Laurent's cousin, a moniker that no one seemed to believe, but everyone accepted. We returned to our seats and waited as ten or fifteen people stood up and told stories of blessings that they had received, or prayers that they needed. We sang. Prayed. Sang. Listened to more of the pastor. Sang. Heard church announcements. Prayed some more. Then, finally, it was over.

And I thought the eleven o'clock service with Mom had been long. I had the ridiculous urge to fly her to Louisiana just so she could sit with me through next week's worship and slip me peppermints during the slow parts.

Next week. The impact of my thoughts hit me at the same time as the sunshine. I stepped out of the barn and lifted my hand, shielding my eyes from the glare of it as I stepped off the bottom step and onto the trampled grass. In a week, would I still be here?

"Let's talk." Laurent's hand closed around my arm and he pulled me forward, striding us toward the truck. I struggled to keep up, surprised at the quick clip of his steps.

He opened the door of the truck, practically shoved me in, and held up a hand to Septime. "Get a ride back with someone."

The order brought me to full alert, the sermon forgotten, and I scooted over into the passenger seat. "What's wrong? Is it Dario? Tell me—"

"Here." He pushed his cell phone out, the screen open, a text message showing. I took it carefully, worried I might hit the wrong button, and read the display.

—Hawk shot. No word yet on condition. Please tell her.

I read it three times, then closed the phone and passed it back to

Laurent. Sitting back, I tried to think through what this meant and how it affected our situation.

Everyone dies. It was probably sacrilegious, but I couldn't help but feel relief.

DARIO

He watched the FBI agent as he adjusted a cheap watch into place.

"Sorry to get you up so soon. I understand that you had a late night."

Dario ignored the comment, glancing at his attorney.

The man smoothed down the front of his suit and lifted one expensive shoe, resting it on his knee in the casual pose of assholes everywhere. "You had news for my client?"

They already knew the news. The beauty of calling half the news outlets in town to document Hawk's arrest? They'd also caught his death. A dozen cameras, shuttering through every bloody minute of it. It'd hit the newswire before Dario had landed. By the time he'd been back in his cell, he knew everything. His ranch foreman, Nick, had shown up and shot Hawk, then been taken down by three slugs in the chest. Another death, caused by Dario's mistakes.

He stared down at the table and listened as the agent recounted everything he already knew. Nick had driven in from the ranch. They found a hotel reservation under his name at the Hampton Inn. He'd shot Hawk with a gun registered in his name. There were a hundred witnesses and camera footage of everything.

"You have any idea why Nick Fentes would want to kill Robert Hawk?"

Dario looked up, his brow furrowing. "Is that a fucking joke?"

His attorney cleared his throat and tapped the table in the sort of warning motion that would get him fired.

Dario tilted his jaw to one side, the muscles in his neck popping, and collected himself, then spelled everything out for the idiot. "Nick and Gwen have been in a relationship for some time. Robert Hawk, directly or indirectly, killed the woman he loved. If I'd had a gun and a death wish, I'd have done the same thing."

He almost *had* done the same thing. In Hawk's home, staring at that chicken shit of evil ... he'd physically struggled with the desire to reach out and wrap his hands around the man's neck, squeezing the cords of tendons until the bones beneath them snapped. Bell had been the only reason he hadn't. Protecting Bell, and the thought of a life with her ... that had kept his temper in check and his hands by his side.

Nick hadn't had that seatbelt to contain him. His world had ended in the same moment that Gwen's had, and Dario hated that he'd been the one who had to tell him. The silence on the other end of that phone... he had felt the heartbreak, had heard the emotion in the hard exhale of breath. Nick hadn't asked who had done it. Dario had told him about Bell, and he had instantly understood, their joint hatred and concern about Robert Hawk a topic that had been discussed at length.

"Are you aware that Nick Fentes has a criminal record?"

Of course, he was. You don't leave your wife alone with a man that you don't know everything about. You don't watch her fall in love without keeping tabs on the situation. It was the same reason that Gwen knew about Meghan, and then Bell. They had loved each other enough to protect each other's hearts. Dario nodded. "Minor stuff. Most of it in his past."

"Larceny and assault aren't exactly minor. He almost killed a man in a bar fight."

Dario shrugged. "You probably come from a good family, Agent King. Solid neighborhood. Honor Roll student. But Nick and I ..."

He leaned forward, resting his forearms on the wooden table, the cheap furniture giving a little under the weight. "I understood where he came from and the situations that led to those arrests. We discussed it, and I felt comfortable hiring him, and knowing that he could handle the ranch and anyone who might show up to mess with it."

Nick could handle Hawk. That was why Dario had hired him. And he had seen Nick's past as a positive, not a negative. The man could fight. Wasn't afraid of getting dirty. He'd gone hungry enough times to appreciate a steady paycheck. He could look at Gwen with a tenderness that went against every other blood vessel in his body. When she was alone at the ranch with Nick, Dario didn't worry about her. He knew that Nick would protect her with his life. And ultimately, the man had.

"We finished the search of Hawk's home. Found something you might find interesting."

Dario kept his expression bored and stayed silent, not reacting when the man reached down and lifted an evidence bag from the banker's box at his feet. Inside the bag was a Smith & Wesson. A gun he recognized. A gun he'd carried out of Bell's suite and into Robert Hawk's home.

He lifted one eyebrow and didn't move, didn't allow himself to think about the moment in the study when he'd planted the gun. The feds had known about the bug. The gun ... that he hadn't told anyone about.

When he'd dropped the gun into the velvet-lined desk drawer, it had made a thud that seemed to echo in the room. He'd looked up and into Hawk's face with the certainty that the man had heard the sound and would walk over to investigate. He'd sweated through the subsequent interaction, sighed with relief when Hawk discovered the wire, and left with a dozen prayers that the weapon would not be discovered until the police searched Hawk's home.

For once, his prayers had been answered.

A gift that, thanks to Nick's swift justice, didn't seem to matter.

"You seen this before?" The man pushed the gun closer and waited. Dario eyed the gun and contemplated his next move.

ELEVEN

BELL

"You trying to git away from me so soon?" Laurent moved between the counter and the fridge, depositing groceries in the efficient manner of a seasoned bachelor.

"Honestly?" I smiled. "Yeah." I pulled a few items out of bags and set them on the counter. "The guy—the one we've been worried about hunting me down, is dead."

At least, he *might* be dead. We hadn't received confirmation of that, though I had practically worn out Laurent's remote by channel surfing news stations. Ridiculously enough, the man didn't have internet OR a smart device. "So... if he *is* dead, then problem solved. Threat vanquished."

"I think you mean vanished." He regarded me with the sober expression of a man actually thinking over the word usage.

"I think either term works. *Please* focus." I leaned against the counter, then stopped when the plastic surface made a sound, something like a crack, from the weight. "I'm about ready to walk home, I'm so ready to get back to Vegas."

And I was. I thought that seeing Dario would give me some peace and patience. Instead, all I had thought about, since he left, was being back in his arms.

He laughed. "You walk out dat door…" He pointed toward the front of the house. "…and you might get fifteen minutes before you be slapping moustiques and jogging back to the air conditioner. Listen." He closed the refrigerator door and turned to me. "Best I am aware, he taking you home." He brushed off his hands. "Okay? Be patient."

A bit of hope bloomed, and I swallowed it, refusing to believe anything until I had hard confirmation and details. "When?"

"I don't know when, but knowing him, he'll call soon. He's probably in the middle of something." He shrugged, moving past me and into the living room. I watched him go and hoped he was right.

DARIO

"Well?" The FBI agent raised his eyebrows.

Dario looked up from the gun. "I've seen a lot of guns in my life-time. I own two that look very similar to that one."

"Not similar, Mr. Capece. Identical. You own a Smith & Wesson that is *identical* to this one. We have the registration for it, right here." He slid a page forward, and Dario didn't follow the move-ment, keeping his gaze tight on the man.

"My guns are locked in a safe in my home, with serial numbers that match their registration. There's no way in hell that gun is mine."

His attorney leaned forward. "Was this the weapon used to kill Gwen Capece?"

Her name caused a pain to stab in Dario's heart, the short syllables a sudden reminder that he would never see her again. He'd never meet her eyes over breakfast and discuss their day. She'd never bitch about the staff, or laugh at his workout regime, or fill up their fridge with disgusting soy milk and wheat germ oil. He swallowed as a vision of her eyes, open and still, blood dotting her cheek, flashed through his mind.

His best friend. *Gone.*

Guilt sat, like a thousand-pound weight in the middle of his chest, pinning him to the seat.

"Yep. Ballistics matched it to the bullet. Anybody have a guess where we found it?" The agent tapped the top of the gun.

Dario stayed silent.

The man waited, and the seconds slowly ticked past before the agent sighed, disappointed in their lack of response. "Fine. Hawk's study. We found the gun in the top drawer of a writing desk."

"I've told you from the beginning that he killed her." And he'd planted the gun as insurance, in case the wire hadn't produced a confession.

The agent scooted forward, his shoes squeaking against the floor. "So, you think Robert Hawk left his mansion at eleven o'clock at night, drove over to The Majestic, waited in a suite you set aside for your girlfriend, then shot his own daughter in the back of the head?" He tilted his head. "Come on, Dario. Those lines don't intersect."

The guy was a fucking idiot if he thought *that* was the scenario in play here. And the guy couldn't be a fucking idiot. Dario kept his mouth shut and fixed his gaze on a point just over the man's shoulder.

"Oh, you're not talking now? You pointed every finger you had at Robert Hawk, and now you're silent?"

He paused, and Dario thought of Bell. Wondered if Laurent had already shared the news of Hawk. He glanced at the clock on the wall and fought the urge to quit this interrogation and call her. He'd fucked all of this up so far. Abandoning her in Louisiana. Not being there for her, at a time when she needed it the most. He'd felt her desperation—had seen the way she had broken down and sobbed.

But he had to keep his distance, and his phone lines free from traceable actions. It wasn't just Hawk he was worried about finding her; it was also this bunch of federal assholes and their idiotic questions.

The FBI agent plowed ahead. "Plus, we've got an alibi. A forty-five-minute phone call between Robert Hawk and his financial advisor, with cell phone triangulation that proves he was in his home during the call."

Another paper slid forward, joining the gun registration. It was a cell phone report, one line highlighted in bright yellow.

"I know what you're thinking. You're about to tell me that he hired someone else and kept his hands clean."

God, this guy was chatty.

Dario leaned forward, ignoring the cell phone report. "I thought we had a common goal in mind—putting Hawk behind bars. Now, your team found the fucking murder weapon in his house, and suddenly you're playing patty cake as if I need to sit down and do your job for you. Isn't happening."

Agent King cleared his throat, folding his hands together as if in prayer. "Let's just calm down for a moment, shall we? I didn't say that you were under suspicion. It's just that..."

He opened the folder and pulled out a series of photos, lining them up in a neat line along the center of the table. Dario watched as the faces were revealed, the driver's license photos of each player in the game.

The agent pointed to the first face in the line. "Nick Fentes. Sleeping with your wife. *Dead.*"

He slid his finger off the cowboy and on to the second photo. "Gwen Capece. Your cheating wife and owner of eighty percent of your marriage's communal assets."

Everything inside Dario flared, each word boiling his blood. *Cheating wife. Owner of eighty percent.* That wasn't what Gwen had been. Those words belonged to another woman, one who didn't wrinkle her nose when she ate cinnamon, or bake cupcakes on Sunday mornings while singing Frank Sinatra. Underneath the table, his hands tightened into fists.

"*Dead.*"

Had he needed to say that word? Did he really think, in the midst of all of this, that Dario had forgotten that fact? The urge to stand, to fist his silk shirt and yank him across the table ... it was unbearable. Dario fixed his eyes on the table, on the blur of photos before him, and blew out a long, controlled breath.

The agent slid his finger from Gwen's delicate features and onto Hawk's distinctive sneer. "Robert Hawk. Father of your wife. Principal of several outstanding real estate loans that you are responsible for and ... if I had to guess ... serious pain in your ass."

The words were said without humor, the final word delivered in a flat tone. "*Dead.*"

Robert Hawk. *Dead.* It was something Dario had wanted for a decade, yet it felt hollow. Still, the confirmation of the news brought his gaze up, past the pointed chin and whiskery lips and to his light brown eyes.

"He's dead?" Dario shifted his legs under the table, stretching them out until they bumped into something. "I thought ... I didn't know there'd been confirmation."

I didn't know the bastard was actually mortal. That's what he felt like saying. With all this time, the fact that such a simple act—a bullet in a parking lot—had felled Hawk ... it seemed too easy. *Why hadn't Dario done it years ago?* But the question to that one was easy. Gwen. Gwen hadn't wanted any harm to befell her father. Gwen had believed that, beneath all of his threats and despicable actions ... that there had been some redeeming characteristics there.

Gwen had been wrong. And now, as a result, she was gone.

The man nodded. "I got the call just before I stepped in here."

Dead, and Nick had done it. Dario felt both cheated and grateful, a contrasting mix of emotions that didn't sit well.

The agent tapped on the second to last photo in the row. "Bell Hartley. Your latest girlfriend and the potential target of the murder. *Missing.*" He said the word as if it meant dead, the suspicion in his voice completely unfounded.

"And then... we have you." He circled his finger around Dario's photo. "Alive. Unscathed. In less than a week, you've gotten rid of your cheating wife, her boyfriend, her meddlesome father, *and* inherited an empire. Forgive me if everything seems a little too clean. Plus, there's the matter of Bell Hartley."

Her name sounded foul on the man's lips, and Dario wanted to reach into his mouth and yank the syllables back. "What *about* Bell Hartley?" Dario growled out the question.

"She's disappeared." The man lifted his chin and fixed Dario with a hard look. "Know anything about that?"

"She's safe. I got her out of town and away from Hawk. That's all you need to know."

"Actually..." The man shifted in his chair. "That's not all we need to know. You can't keep leaving us in the dark and then expecting us to jump when you snap your fingers. The FBI doesn't work like that. When you lied to the police and told them that was Bell's body in that condo—you brought her into this mess. The fact that she's your girlfriend, and you've got a dead wife on your hands ... that doesn't help anything as far as you are concerned."

Dario sat back in the chair and folded his arms. "Fine. You want Bell? I'll bring in Bell. You can ask her whatever you want."

The man studied him, his finger tapping a slow beat against the desk. "Thank you, Mr. Capece, for that permission. Not that we need it.

"You need it if you plan on finding her."

The edges of the man's mouth turned down. "We are, I assure you, quite skilled in that art." He leaned back and buttoned the top button of his coat. "Finding people is what we do, Mr. Capece."

"Well, not to measure dicks or anything, but that stack of missing girls' posters says otherwise."

Dario leaned forward and tapped the stack of manila folders, his face hardening into a scowl. "I didn't plan on Bell joining their ranks. You'll have to forgive anything I did to keep that possibility at bay."

The man raised an eyebrow. "Anything? That's a strong word, Dario."

It wasn't. *Anything* was a weak word where she was concerned. Anything didn't begin to cover the enormity of what he would do to protect her. Anything sat in nine-to-five cubicles, it played inside the lines and lived with modern society. *Everything* was a far better word. He'd do everything to protect her and burn down this town if that's what it took. Planting the gun ... hiding her away ... it was all just the surface of what he was capable of.

"I feel like we are getting off track." The attorney jumped in, anxious to justify his eight-hundred-dollars-an-hour rate.

The agent pointed that stupid finger back in Dario's direction. "You mentioned that you could bring Bell Hartley in. Do it. We want to talk to her, to get her statement on what happened that night. And in the meantime, with this murder weapon in hand and no longer any need to mislead Robert Hawk, you're free to go. But our investigation is still ongoing. As I said, this is a very convenient turn of events for you, Mr. Capece. All of your problems have suddenly found themselves in the morgue and off of your plate."

"Gwen was never a problem of mine." Dario's voice broke on the truth of the words. "And neither was Nick. Robert Hawk is the only one in this lot I wished ill of. But I didn't want *that*."

He stood. "Being shot to death was too easy a death for him. I wanted him sentenced. I wanted his crimes exposed, those girls' bodies found, answers and guilt assigned. I wanted him to answer for what he did, and for him to admit to the world that he killed his only daughter. You think I'm happy this happened? You think this is *convenient* for me? *Fuck* that. I want my wife back. I want to put her on that ranch, in that cowboy's arms, and for her to have the life she deserved—one free of a sadistic and tyrannical man who called himself her father. I want to take my *girlfriend* and have a normal fucking relationship with her, one where she doesn't have to change her cell phone number, or hide in a million-dollar suite with me instead of going on a proper date. I want the freedom, for once, to live my life without that puppet master yanking on every string."

He stopped, his breath coming hard, repressed emotions bubbling to the surface. This was bad. He was stronger than this. More controlled. More *in* control. "You tell me again that this is convenient, and I'll break your fucking neck."

He glared at the agent, willing him to open that scrawny throat, to poke at him *one* more time ... but the man didn't. He stayed quiet, and Dario turned and reached for the door handle, anxious to find a phone and call Bell.

TWELVE

BELL

For three hours, I continued to channel surf and watched the same videos over and over. Nick Fentes, shoving through the crowd. Gunshots. People running. A blurry look at a fallen Robert Hawk, the camera shoved out of the way. I watched reporters go through Nick Fentes history, his arrest record, and an interview with his childhood next door neighbor. When my phone finally sounded, the Vegas area code flashing across the small black Nokia screen, I jerked to my feet. "Hello?"

I'd expected Dario's voice, and my elation sank, then warbled back to life, when I recognized the voice at the other end. *Lance.*

"Hey B."

"Lance. What's..." I forced my voice to stay calm, tried for a sunny version of my old self, and failed miserably. "What's up?"

"Damn, it's good to hear your voice. Your boy gave me this number, wanted me to make sure you're alright. He's at the police station, but said he'd call in a few hours. I guess the danger's passed?"

I shrugged, then realized he couldn't see me. "Maybe. I mean, we were worried about Hawk." I walked into the kitchen, moving away from the television's noise.

"We've missed you, babe. Brit is twice as grouchy without you, Rick doesn't know how to fetch his own fucking Sprite, and customers are blaming your absence for their bad luck."

I smiled at the sheer normalcy of the comments, grateful for their distraction. "Their bad luck increases your profit."

He laughed. "I know that shit, but don't tell them. Where are you? Are they taking good care of you?"

Laurent had strips of beef jerky drying on the counter, and I broke off a piece and popped it in my mouth. "I'm in the middle of nowhere. You'd probably love it here. There's all sorts of stuff to take your Hummer through."

"Any single women?"

I thought of Septime and smiled. "I've met one. But I'm not sure you're man enough for her."

He scoffed and made a stupid comment about penis size. I ignored it and pulled a glass from the cabinet, filling it with water from the sink.

"By the way, your boyfriend's a *complete* pain in the ass. He gave me a whole list of things to do."

I heard the crinkle of paper and imagined him driving, squinting at the page as he wove through lanes of traffic.

"What's on your to-do list?"

"Let's see. Go by your parent's house. They're worried about you. I'm pretty sure your dad's going to cut my dick off if you don't get home in one piece. Oh, and I called Meredith. That chick doesn't shut up. She's also concerned—all of your roommates are. This week has been hell on everybody. And it doesn't help that the police have been asking everyone questions."

A knot formed, twisted, and yanked in my gut.

"Questions? Like what?"

He snorted. "Everything. Random shit. How long you've been seeing Dario. What you're like as an employee…how much money you make…whether we think you're capable of murder."

Part of the beef jerky lodged in my throat. "They think *I* killed Gwen?"

"Who knows. I'm not exactly surprised that the mistress—no offense, B—is a suspect when the wife is murdered. Vegas PD isn't going to miss that fluorescent yellow possibility. Just like they aren't writing Dario off their list of suspects."

Dario. Just the sound of his name and my chest grew warmer. "He didn't do it."

He said nothing, and I sensed his suspicion in the silence.

"He *didn't* do it. Trust me. I was there. I saw him, his reaction—" I broke off the sentence, the memory sweeping over me, as painful as it had been the last time it hit. The way his voice had pitched, the awful cry of her name, the sounds of him sobbing. The last time I'd heard a man cry like that … it'd been when I told my father what had happened at the barn. When the police had ignored him. When he'd swung his fist at the wall and missed. When he'd wanted to kill Johnny and his father but been too drunk to drive over and do it. He'd cried through all of it, and the sounds had broken my heart and stacked up the guilt.

Dario had loved Gwen. If I didn't know it before, I had realized it then, in that suite, the Vegas lights glittering in the background, her

94

legs sliding forward as he had gathered her to his chest. The pinched look of his features when he had staggered toward me. The cold, businesslike air that had shuttered into place when he'd spoken to me.

It'd been a different man who had come to me two days ago. The one who had lifted me off the stairs and carried me inside? The one who had whispered my name as he had thrust inside of me, his body framing me, touch protecting me, kiss soothing me ... he had been mine. Healed, slightly. Guilty, still.

But not guilty for what Lance was suspecting him for. He was guilty —we both were—of trigger events that had caused her murder. But we'd been innocent of intent, a distinction that didn't seem to matter. She was still dead.

I lifted the glass to my forehead and pressed the cool side of it against my skin, taking a deep breath. I tried to remember what my mother had said, the words she had preached to me when I had struggled after the rape.

It wasn't my fault.

They were the evil ones.

God knew the truth.

I was a victim, but I didn't have to act like one.

I had done nothing wrong.

It wasn't my fault.

God, I needed her. I needed to tell her everything and have her tell me what to do. I needed to have her hug me, and comfort me, and to convince me that this was *not my fault. Not Dario's fault.*

Only, it was.

I wasn't an innocent farm girl, alone in a barn, just after dark.

I had followed lust and emotion and disregarded safety, ethics, and the seventh freaking commandment. I just hadn't believed the true evil of the psychopath lurking in the wings.

"B? You there?"

I brought the glass to my lips and took a deep sip, downing half of it before coming up for air. "Yeah. I'm here. When are you going to my parents?"

"Tonight. I've got to run by The House and take care of a few things, then I'll hit the road. I just called and let them know I was coming. Your mom's got lasagna in the oven now."

Lasagna. I could almost smell it. Homesickness hit, and I set the glass down before I dropped it. "They don't know about Dario. Not ... everything. I don't know what they know, or what the police have told them." The awareness of how little I knew sank like a rock in my gut. I felt a dozen steps behind, ignorant to everything and being fed information through an eye-dropper when I needed an IV.

"Don't worry about it, B. Keep yourself safe. I'll see you soon."

No. Don't hang up. Don't. I need to hear your voice for more than that. I struggled to find something to say, a question to ask him, an excuse to prolong the conversation. I needed, for just another moment, to feel normal.

I was too slow. He hung up the phone and I took a deep, wet breath, struggling to hold in the tears.

THIRTEEN

Frogs apparently, at nightfall, don't shut the hell up. I sat on the back step, my arms wrapped around my knees, and listened to them. It was a concert of sounds, almost beautiful in their varieties.

I swiped at a mosquito and resisted the urge to glance at my phone. I pictured Lance, on his way home from my parents' house, his stomach packed with gooey hot lasagna. Mom made the best lasagna. Five layers high. Four types of cheese. Packed with enough sausage and beef to make you roll over on the couch and belch in satisfaction.

I, on the other hand, had a microwave hot dog for dinner. Thirty seconds on high, the skinny dog wrapped in a napkin, and a little wrinkly when I pulled it from the microwave. Dipped in ketchup and mustard and washed down with some ginger ale. It actually hadn't been *that* bad. Had it not been competing with Ma's lasagna, I probably would have enjoyed it.

"Hey." Laurent's boots shook the wooden porch, and I looked over my shoulder and up at him, perking up at the phone he held out. "It's da big man. For you."

I pushed to my feet and grabbed the phone from his hand. "Thank you."

Turning away, I lifted the phone to my ear. "Hey."

"Hey, love." He sounded tired, the vowels gruff, but there was a lilt in the greeting, something that gave me hope. "Ready to come home?"

I squealed, jumping a little in place at the unexpected gift. "Yes. Now. Immediately. When?"

"I've got to meet with the funeral director first thing in the morning, then I'll head to the airport. I'll be there by one or two, your time."

I nodded. "I'll be ready."

He chuckled, and I wished I could see it, could see the stretch of those beautiful features, the glint of his grin, the way his eyes warmed, and he looked at me as if I alone held the key to his happiness.

"Are you okay, Bell?"

It was the wrong question at the wrong time, the tender concern in his voice puncturing my dam of control.

I pinched my eyes shut and fought to maintain my composure. "I'm fine." The last word whispered out of me, trembling in its delivery, and he would have had to be deaf not to hear it.

"I'm going to make everything right. When you—when we come back here—I'll do everything right. Take care of you. Protect you. You're going to want for *nothing*, do you understand that?"

It was a desperate question, his control wobbling, and the man still didn't understand what made me tick. He still waved money and finery in the same fist as love and comfort, not recognizing the value in his presence. I wanted *him*. I wanted his love. His time. His attention. Nothing else.

"Do you *understand?* This isn't like before. Everything has changed now."

"Yes."

Everything has changed now. He was right. No Gwen. No Hawk. I would go back to Vegas with him and ... my mind tried to grasp the idea of what my new reality would be.

What was a single Dario like? How would he be as a boyfriend? His wife had just *died*. What emotional capacity, if any, would he have? And he had just been accused of murdering his wife. Without a trial or proof of Robert Hawk's guilt, the paparazzi—and the public opinion— would follow him, and us, everywhere.

Everything has changed now. He said it like it was a good thing, but standing in the damp heat of a Louisiana night, Laurent's phone pressed to my ear ... I wanted a moment where everything went back to how it had been. Careless sexual chemistry. Late night texts. Butterflies and forbidden moments.

Everything has changed now.

"I love you. I'll see you tomorrow."

"I love you too."

He paused, and I could feel the weight of the silence, the press of some unasked question hanging between us. I waited, but he only told me goodbye, and we hung up.

I took a deep breath, then went to tell Laurent the news.

The airport was eerily familiar. Still deserted. Still broken pavement and a chain-link fence. When I was last here, I'd stumbled off that plane, afraid and intimidated further by the giant man who met me there. Now, I stood next to Laurent, staring out at the sunny runway, and breathed in the familiar scent of his soap.

"Thank you. For everything." I fought the urge to hug him. It would be awkward, most definitely. He'd probably untangle my arms and step away. Or stand stick straight and pat my back with the sort of motion you reserve for elderly grandmothers. I looked back to the runway and tucked my hands into my back pockets instead. "I know I was a total pain in the ass."

He shrugged. "You was."

I laughed, and a dragonfly buzzed away, as if surprised by the sound.

Laurent shifted, started to speak, then stopped himself. I waited, curious about what he was struggling to get out.

"Let me tell you a little bit about our boy. This wasn't a small thing, sending you here. And right now, he probably feels a little broken. This isn't the first time he's lost someone he's close to, someone that he felt responsible to take care of."

He leaned forward and spat in the dirt. "You know, Dario lost his Momma as a teenager."

I nodded.

"He didn't handle it well. All but killed himself on alcohol and loose women, got locked up half a dozen times before he was able to figure himself out."

He glanced at me. "This time, he's handling it da best that he can. And he's doing a lot betta than I thought. But it's going to be hard on him, Gwen's daddy dying like that. It takes away Dario's ability to handle the situation. He's going to feel cheated. So go easy on him. Be *patient* with him."

"He loved her." I swallowed, my pride struggling with the right words. "It's hard for me, seeing that—"

"Easy now." He pulled me in front of him, making me look him square in the eyes. "It was a different sort of love, what he had for her. I've known that man since I was a babe, grew up next to him. I've never known him to really fall for a woman before. He hadn't ever let 'emself do that, or never found da right woman."

I looked away from him and he tightened his grip on my shoulders. I reluctantly brought my gaze back to his face.

"But he's acting different with you. I've been watching what he's doing. He spent a long time making that life with Gwen and hadn't veered off that path for thirteen years, now. For him to have risked it, for him to still be chasing you down and sticking by your side? That not the Dario I know. That a different man. So?" He shrugged. "Maybe it be love. Maybe you the one for him. I hadn't seen enough of you together. But he coulda sent you anywhere to be protected. He sent you *here*, to his home. He's fought for you in that hell of a city and risked being locked up over it. And now he's coming back to get ya, the first chance he get. Those are big steps for our big man."

We heard it then, the faint drone that grew louder. I lifted my chin and stared at the sky, finding the moving lights, the dip of the plane as it curved toward the runway. I shook free of Laurent and stepped out onto the open pavement, and watched his approach, wondering if he could see me.

Laurent's words followed me, hummed in my ears, even as the plane drew closer, its engine louder, my clothes beginning to press against my body from the force of the wind.

I had viewed being here as a curse. But maybe, instead, it had been a blessing. A sign of Dario's love.

The plane coasted down, bouncing slightly on the runway before touching the ground, the noise deafening, the force of the wind flattening my hair across my face, the dark strands tangling in my mouth and nose. I pushed them away and turned back to Laurent.

"THANK YOU!" I called out the words and he nodded. I stepped forward, unable to resist, and flung my arms around him, gripping him tightly in a hug.

He handled it well. No polite taps on the shoulder. No stiff stillness. He squeezed me carefully, then released me. "You take care of yourself. And him."

I stepped away. "I will." Turning, I jogged to meet the plane.

DARIO

He could see her through the fogged glass of the King Air. Hair whipping in the wind. Arms tightly crossed over her abdomen. She stopped and waited, her head turning to face into the breeze. The sight of her was almost painful. He'd felt the same way a few days ago, hidden in Laurent's truck, watching her talk to him on the phone. Every movement she'd made had been a tug on his heart, his guilt, his need.

What if he lost her, too? How would he handle it? How could he continue?

The fear was so intense he almost pushed away, had attempted to fight for distance during this last week, had struggled to find his ground—one separate from her.

But he couldn't. His fear was intermingled with love—or caused by it. The stronger the fear grew, the stronger the love became. His only option was to remove all risks. Keep her safe, treat her like a queen, win her heart. Go all in, and hope that luck, for just this one time, was in his favor.

The plane settled to a stop, the locks disengaging, and he pushed himself out of the seat and forced the heavy door open. The airlock broke, and the humidity rushed in, bringing with it the familiar scent of pollen and swamp. He cranked it fully open and unfolded the steps, jumping over them in his haste to get on the ground and into her arms.

When they met, her hug had the strength of a tiger. She gripped him fiercely, and their lips met. Collided. Melted.

He wrapped his arms around her, lifting her off the ground, his mouth greedy on hers, sucking, kissing, nipping at her lips. He had missed her taste, her fire, her need. The warmth of her hug, the give of her body, the shine in those eyes. He pulled away and stared down at her, memorizing every inch of her delicate features.

So beautiful. So strong. *His*. He would learn. He'd learn to love her without restraint, without the fear of evil lurking, without the many facades and lies.

She was his future.

FOURTEEN

BELL

Peace. I rested my head on his thigh and looked up at him. In the dark interior of the plane, he was all shadows and outlines, rugged sexuality hidden just enough to drive me crazy.

He looked down at me and smiled. "I've missed you."

He ran his hand through my hair, carefully untangling the strands and I closed my eyes at the sensation, stretching my legs out across the bench seat until my toes hit the cool exterior wall. The plane rocked a little, and I felt my stomach pitch in response. I put a hand on my belly. I should have skipped the pork rinds on the drive over.

"Where are we going?"

"Good question." He shifted a little underneath me, and I almost mewled in pleasure when the tips of his fingers gently ran across my scalp. "I don't know where to go. I haven't been back home since—

since Gwen died." His fingers stopped their journey, and I looked up at him.

"I can't go back in that penthouse. She's everywhere in it. And I can't even stand to be in the building. With what almost happened to you..." He shook his head. "It's tainted."

"But you have other homes, right? Somewhere else you can stay?"

He nodded, his eyes on me. "Yeah. We own—"

He stopped and swore, pulling his gaze away from me and looking out the window, the night sky illuminating the unshaved line of his jaw. I'd never seen him with facial hair before, and I reached up, running my fingers along the soft scruff of it. I watched as his Adam's apple bobbed, control shuttering back over his features.

"I," he amended quietly. "There's a dozen other properties *I* own, hotels and casinos. Finding a suite isn't a problem. But I'd rather find something without a history. Someplace we can stay that's secure, at least to ride out the next few weeks."

I pushed myself off of his lap and into an upright position.

"You want to move in together?"

He had the audacity to look hurt. "You don't?"

"I—"

I didn't know what I wanted. I didn't want to be apart from him but wanted my independence. Moving in with him seemed like a giant step forward in a relationship that was barely past infancy. I pointed this out, and he frowned.

"I think we passed infancy back in San Diego. And with everything that has happened since..." He reached out and pulled me closer, lifting me onto his lap.

My head brushed against the top of the ceiling and I ducked a little, laughing despite myself. "This plane isn't exactly designed for canoodling."

He pulled on my neck, brought my mouth to his, and I forgot my next words. My mouth opened—hungry—and he met my tongue with his. God, he knew how to kiss. He dominated me while still teasing, his hand digging into my hair, holding my head in place as he gently sucked on my lip, bruised over my tender skin and soothed it all with one talented swipe of his tongue. I relaxed into his hold, trusting him, needing him, each kiss another stitch holding me together.

I needed *more*. More touching, more contact, more of him. I broke away from his kiss and glanced over my shoulder. Behind us, a row of seats faced backward, the back of the pilot's head was visible just past the headrests. I returned my attention to him, reaching down and pulling at the soft waistband of his workout pants.

He read my mind and shook his head at me, his eyes growing darker. I slid my hand under the fabric, along the hot surface of his skin, and smiled when my fingers made contact with his cock. He hissed when I gripped him, already hard, already needy—a status that only fueled my intent. I worked my fist along his shaft and watched the drug of arousal steal over his features. *Yes.*

"Bell..." He whispered my name, and it was both a plea and a protest. I ignored the protest and slid my grip to the base of his shaft, admiring the length and girth of it. God, he was beautiful. His thick shaft, a smooth, perfect head, and the ability to swell and stiffen at just the touch of my fingers.

"I need this," I whispered.

It was stupid of me to wear jeans. I should have been like him, in loose pants that could quickly be pulled away. Instead, I had on skinny jeans that would take a surgical team to peel off.

"I've *missed* this." I leaned forward, and he lifted his chin to meet me, this kiss slower, his mouth distracted with the increased action of my hand. I broke away and glanced back at the pilot.

"Ignore him. Kiss me again."

I didn't argue. I leaned forward and met his lips, feeling the catch of his breath when I rolled my thumb over his head.

The plane continued, the pilot ignored us, and the cabin heated up as I worked my hand faster, and his grip on me tightened.

"I see what you did there." Dario squeezed my knee.

I turned toward him and repositioned the pillow, stifling a yawn. "What did I do?"

Behind him, sun pierced through the window. I tilted my head to the side so his profile blocked the glare.

"You tried to distract me with sex."

"That wasn't sex. It was a hand job. One-sided pleasure." I stuck out my tongue at him, and he smiled.

"I'll rectify that situation the moment I get you out of those jeans."

The yawn came back, and I lost the battle, reaching up my hand to cover the gesture. "That extraction process will probably have to wait. I'm exhausted."

He ran his hand along my legs, squeezing the muscles as he went. "Why don't you want to move in with me?"

"It's not that I don't—" I stopped myself. "I do." I shifted lower in the seat. "I've just never done that with anyone I've dated before."

"I'm not certain you've ever had a real relationship before."

A valid point, but not one I was ready to admit. "It's still a big step for me. I just need to marinate on it for a day or so."

He nodded, and I could see how exhausted he was. My feelings of guilt, my depression, and struggle over the last few days... his had to be so much worse. And yet, he hadn't had time to recover. He'd been in jail and confronting Hawk, working with police, and flying cross-country to see me.

I pressed a kiss gently against his forehead and he closed his eyes. "Okay," I whispered.

His eyes opened. "Okay, what?"

"I marinated." I smiled. "I'm ready."

When we stepped off the plane, they were waiting. A string of FBI windbreakers, moving forward as if I was wanted for treason. I hesitated at the top of the plane's steps, and Dario nudged me.

"It's okay. I promise."

I took the steps carefully and was met at the bottom by a man with a bushy mustache.

"Bell Hartley?" He eyed me carefully, examining my outfit as if it might hold evidence. While I had been wearing these jeans the night Gwen was killed, any evidence from them was probably in Laurent's lint filter right now.

"Yes?"

"We have some questions for you." he gestured behind him, to a dark navy eighteen-passenger. "If you could please come with us."

"She'll meet you at the field office," Dario interrupted. "Or the station, wherever you prefer. *With* her attorney."

The man's gaze moved to mine, a question mark in them. I nodded.

"For your own safety, Ms. Hartley. We'd prefer you to ride with us—"

"No." I shook my head. "I'd rather not." I leaned against Dario, and his hand tightened on my waist.

The man studied both of us, then nodded.

My second experience in a police station went more smoothly than the first. It still took three hours, I still told the same stories four different times, and still had to be photographed and fingerprinted. But no one scoffed at me, and this time I had an attorney. She was an asshole, but she was my asshole, and half-way through the questioning, I relaxed, secure in the knowledge that she had everything under control. When I finally walked out, I leaned on Dario for physical and emotional support.

"How'd you do?" He wrapped his arms around me.

"She did great." The attorney spoke, and Dario looked to me for confirmation.

I nodded. "It wasn't bad. They weren't happy that I skipped town, and I've been told not to do that again without telling them."

"Fuck them," Dario responded, leaning forward and giving me a kiss. "Let's get you home. You look exhausted."

Just the suggestion of sleep caused me to yawn. He chuckled, then reached out and shook the attorney's hand. 'Thanks."

She nodded. "I'll be in touch if anything changes."

"Make sure it doesn't." He opened my car door and I sank into the seat.

"So... you're staying *here*." Meredith peered up at Dario as if he was an unknown specimen, one she planned to slice off a piece of and stick it under her microscope. I interrupted her inspection with a hug, the third one I'd given her since walking into the house.

"Yep." Dario drawled out the word, looking too big in the living room. I gave Meredith a look of warning and headed for the bedroom.

"What?" She widened her eyes in innocence. "It's just a little odd. Like that dork from Papa John's sticking a Djorno in the oven." She followed us down the hall without shame. "I mean, don't you own, like, five hotels?"

"Something like that," Dario responded.

"Exactly. And isn't each hotel full of... I don't know...." She looked up at the ceiling as if searching for a constellation. "Rooms? Beds? Places to put that ginormous head of yours?"

"Yo, yo, yoooooo." Jackie wandered down the hall in SpongeBob SquarePants pajama bottoms and stopped short when she saw Dario. "Oh. Hel-lo."

Dario cocked his head at me. "I'm rethinking the hotel."

"You should." Jackie turned to Meredith with a frown. "Do you have any Azo? I've got a bitch of a UTI that's burning a hole through my catheter."

"Check the cabinet by the microwave," Meredith said.

"So... we're just going to go to bed." I pushed open my door and ushered Dario inside before he knew all four of our menstrual cycles.

"I missed you, B." Jackie sidled inside before I got the door closed and wrapped her UTI-infested arms around me. I grudgingly accepted the hug, then motioned her toward the door. She winked at Dario and strolled toward the door with the speed of a drunk caterpillar.

"And... you're staying *here*." Meredith repeated the statement for the fifth or sixth time since he stepped in the front door.

I intervened. "YES. He owns lots of hotel rooms. He's staying here in this loony, infection riddled, house. He's Papa John with an annoying cast of roommates. Now GO AWAY."

I pushed her as gently as I could manage and swung the door shut, the action blocked by her foot. I pushed the door harder, and her eyes narrowed. Her toes must be pure steel. Funny that I never noticed that before, at all our movie nights and pedicure parties.

"Be careful, B." She said the words so softly I almost missed them.

I met her eyes and fought the urge to give her another hug. *Be careful?* I didn't even know how to go about doing that. "This week, you and me. Lunch?"

She smiled. "Sushi at Transit?"

I nudged her foot with the door, and she reluctantly moved it. "It's a date."

"Oh, Bell?"

Something in her voice caused me to stop. I raised my eyebrows, and she grinned at me.

"You might wanna check the fridge before you head to bed."

I watched her go, then turned to see Dario, in the middle of my room, one of my pillows in hand. My stomach growled, a reminder that I hadn't eaten since before our flight.

He caught my expression. "What?"

"Don't get comfortable yet." I reached for his hand and pulled him toward the kitchen. If my instincts were right, he wouldn't want to miss this.

FIFTEEN

"Fuck me."

"I can't take anymore."

"Just suck it off."

Meredith stopped in the doorway to the kitchen and crossed her arms. "Are you guys fucking or eating?"

Dario turned toward her, a fork in hand, pierced into a wedge of lasagna. "Have you *tasted* this?" He held it out to her. "It's insane. Better than Bartellos."

She smirked. "Uh... yeah? It's Momma Hartley's. Best lasagna on the planet." She stole his fork and stuck the bite in her mouth. "You don't know what I've had to do to keep Jackie and Lydia away from this. It's been the freaking Hunger Games, trying to hold them at bay."

I blew her a kiss and tried, unsuccessfully, to take one final bite. I lifted the fork, paused in front of my mouth, then set it back down. "I can't. Dario?"

He waved me off, leaning back in the chair to stretch. I heard the wood creak, and Meredith and I both eyed the Target special with skepticism.

I stood, reaching for the paper plates and tossing them in the trash. I grabbed the Saran Wrap and Meredith stopped me.

"You guys go to bed. I'll wrap up what's left."

"Thanks. I love you."

She smiled and pulled me in for another hug. "I love you too."

Dario bumped into the table when he stood, and the view of him in our cramped kitchen was comical. I stifled a smile and headed for the bedroom, feeling him close behind me, the gentle run of his fingers along the small of my back. We stopped at my bedroom door, and I looked back at him, his large frame blocking out the hall light, a smile stretching across his face as he dropped his head and kissed me.

"Come on." I pushed open the door and pulled him inside. "Let's go to bed."

He was too long for the mattress. I pulled my pajama top on and stared at his feet, which hung off the end.

He caught my look and groaned, rolling onto his side, the bed frame squeaking loudly in response.

"Don't look at me like that. If it were up to me, we'd be in a Ritz Carlton."

It was true. We'd actually had a reservation, one made somewhere above Vegas, for a presidential suite with a jacuzzi tub. But when we'd touched down, and I'd stepped off the plane and inhaled the familiar dry air of the desert ... I'd only wanted to go home. I'd wanted to see Meredith. I'd wanted my pajamas and my face wash and my bed with the marigold sheets and fuzzy pillows. My queen bed that was currently *dying* under the additional weight of him.

I buttoned the front of my pajamas and reconsidered the Ritz Carlton reservation.

As soon as we'd gotten in the car, I'd broached the idea of taking me home. He'd made a number of excellent points that included words like *room service*, *morning massages*, and *personal butler*. I'd held firm to my desire to sleep in my own bed, using my own words like *middle of the freaking swamp* and *I have the vagina so I make the rules*. He finally conceded, but only under the agreement that he stayed with me. It was easy to agree to. I didn't want to leave his side, and my fear hadn't dissolved entirely. Sure, Robert Hawk was dead. But did that completely remove the threat?

It seemed too good to be true—the sudden ability to continue our relationship without any repercussions.

I pulled back the cover and snorted at the limited space between him and the edge of the bed.

"You're going to push me off."

"I would *never* push you off." He delivered the promise with the solemn oath of a choir boy hiding a stolen toy behind his back. "Fuck you off the bed? Maybe." He grinned.

I crawled onto the mattress, sliding under the covers and against his hard, warm body. "I ate enough lasagna to bust the stomach of a pig. So did you. No one is fucking anyone off any bed tonight. Plus..." I yawned, for the twentieth time that night. "I can barely keep my eyes open as it is."

He rolled me over until my back was to his chest, us both on our sides, and cupped me against his body. "Fine. We won't break the bed tonight. But soon. Tomorrow."

I smiled. "I'll put it on the calendar."

He gently nibbled on my shoulder, the scruff of his beard tickling me, and I squirmed. "Stop. Go to bed. I mean it."

"Fine." He kissed the spot, and I felt the pillow settle as he laid his head down. "You need a longer bed." He stage-whispered the words, and I ignored them, a smile playing across my lips. "I'll buy you one tomorrow. With more pillows. And night lights. I need a night light."

At *that* ridiculous statement, I pulled at the closest pillow and swung it around, the cotton connecting with his shoulder with a loud slap.

He growled, stealing it from me, and threw his leg over mine, trapping me in his embrace. "Stop talking and let me sleep. It's hard enough without a night light."

My torso shook with an attempt to contain my laughter. "I don't like you." My words cracked in their attempt at severity.

"No, you don't." He nuzzled my neck and planted a kiss on my shoulder. "You love me."

I said nothing, but it was true. He squeezed me gently, a warm cocoon of strong muscles, steady heartbeats, and soft kisses. *God, I'd missed his arms. His touch. The way he held me. I felt safe.*

"How did you like Louisiana?"

I turned at the question, shifting so I could see his face. "You mean, other than being apart from you?"

"Yeah. Other than that."

"I don't know..." I shrugged, trying to think of something nice to say about the place he grew up in. "I stayed at Laurent's house all the time. Except for the one time we went to church."

He groaned. "Oh god. The big white barn?"

I laughed. "You know it?"

"Are you kidding?" He tucked a piece of hair behind my ear, his gaze moving over my smile. "Every Sunday while my mother was alive. Those two-hour sermons were my own personal hell."

I winced. "I think that's blasphemous."

"Trust me." He leaned over and gently nipped at my nose. "God himself was bored in that barn."

I smiled at the image of a young Dario, in a button-up shirt and khaki pants, sitting beside his mother in the pew. My grin faded. "I wish I could have met your mother."

"Yeah." He settled onto his side. "I wish you could have too. She would have loved you."

He'd lost so much in his life. Both parents. His life in Louisiana. And now Gwen. He gathered me to his chest, his touch tender, and all I wanted, was to give him everything back. Erase all the pain. Heal his future. Our future. Which was a giant fuzzy blur of a concept at this time.

I loved him. And that unknown future of *us* terrified me.

Something jutted against my hip. Something hard. It pushed against me, then retreated.

I felt the drag of it down the back of my thigh and giggled against the pillow when it moved in between my legs. "Stop."

The mattress shifted, and I opened one eye to see a hand braced on the bed next to my head. It was a good hand. Strong, long fingers. Short clipped nails. Muscular. Tan. The cords of his wrists flexed and I felt the unexpected burst of hot air against my ear.

"Good morning."

God, his voice in the morning. Thick. Gruff. If you put that *good morning* on a pancake, women would be orgasming their way through IHOP. His lips softly closed on my earlobe and tugged, the sensation traveling all the way through my body and down to my toes. *Now*, I was awake.

He lowered his body, that forearm flexing, and I felt that hard, insistent cock push in between my legs, my pajama pants creating a madding barrier that needed to be removed, immediately. I reached down, squirming to find the room to move, and worked the drawstring pants over my hips.

He didn't help. He lifted his hips off me, held up his weight with his hands, and did nothing.

I huffed in exasperation. "Can't you help me here?"

He chuckled, leaning down to place a kiss in between my shoulder blades. "And ruin this view? Nah."

I'm not sure what kind of view existed, me flopping around on my stomach like a beached whale, but I got the pants to mid-thigh and stopped, collapsing on the bed, my hands sliding back to their place under the pillow. "There. Ravage me."

"Shhhh. You're ruining it."

His right hand moved. I felt the brush of fingers against my bare ass, then the firm, confident slide of those digits in between my thighs. "Part your legs a little."

I parted, my knees digging into the covers, and almost lifted off the bed when he pushed his finger inside.

"God, you're so responsive." He withdrew, spread my cheeks slightly, and lined up his cock. Paused.

"I don't have a condom."

"It's okay. Just give it to—"

I lost the words the moment he thrust inside, a thick intrusion that felt so different. Skin to skin. Thick and throbbing, bare and perfect. He pushed fully in, dragged slowly out, and I flexed my inner muscles, clenching him.

He let out a string of filthy curses, the words hissing through clenched teeth. "God, you feel..."

He sat back on his knees, his hands spreading my ass cheeks, and I looked over my shoulder, watching him. His focus was on our meeting, the view of his thick cock sliding in. "I wish you could see how perfect you look, stretched around my dick. So pink. So wet. So fucking delicious."

He tilted his head and met my eyes. Slowed his movement and then quickened his strokes. I closed my eyes and let out a low groan. Felt the bite of his fingers into my ass. Heard the grunt of his effort. My nipples stood on end, the rut of him see-sawing them across the mattress, the combination of slick bare flesh and sounds building a crescendo that hummed along my skin.

Sunlight. There was the cool air of exposure as he turned me over, pulling off my pants and lowering his body between my legs. He thrust back inside and I wrapped my legs around his muscular waist, my hands exploring the landscape of his chest, his shoulders, his arms. His mouth found mine, his kiss claiming me, swallowing my gasp as he drove fully in. God, had anyone ever filled me so much? Had anyone ever gotten so deep? He broke from my kiss and held his weight with one hand, his other thumbing open the front buttons of my pajama top. He spread open the sides, baring my breasts, his hand reverently moving over the curves.

"So beautiful, Bell."

I arched under his touch, my nipples aching for stimulation, each rough brush of his finger causing a twinge between my legs. He pinched one, and I moaned. He slid his hand up further, wrapping it around my neck, and I dug my heels into him, fucking him from the bottom. His eyes darkened, holding mine tightly, gauging my reactions. I reached my hand up and placed it over his, squeezing.

"Dirty girl."

Everything quickened. His thrusts. My breath. The pleasure climbing upward toward my orgasm.

I panted through the hold he had on my neck. "Tighter."

He tightened his grip and every sensation sharpened. The pound of his cock. The scrap of my nails against his chest. The bite of his teeth on my shoulder. Pushing so deep into me. So thick. So fast. I gulped for air, my eyes closing, everything darkening.

"I'm about—"

The orgasm split me into pieces, a searing jolt of pleasure that took me apart in a blinding burst of sensation. I seized around him, my eyes snapping open, everything spinning, exploding, dissolving. He released my neck, his mouth covering mine, and he stole a kiss at the moment before he cursed, coming inside of me, his orgasm loud and long, beautiful to watch, beautiful to experience, and all mine.

SIXTEEN

Jackie and Lydia stared at Dario as if they'd never seen a man before. A big, sexy, Italian man—one sitting at the table and eyeing a microwaved Eggo as if it were foreign matter.

"These are ... blueberries?" He tilted the Eggo to one side and peered at it.

"They're chocolate chips." Lydia intoned.

I closed the fridge door and reached over, pulling it off his fork with my hand and holding it out to him. "No one eats them on a fork. What are you, Mr. Fancy Pants? I saw where you're from. Laurent used a *clothesline* for God's sake."

He grinned at me and stood, pulling the waffle from my hand and giving me a kiss. He tore off a chunk of the Eggo and chewed. "There. Happy?"

He grimaced and made a big production of swallowing. "Yummy."

I rolled my eyes and plucked the rest of it from his fingers. "God, you're a snob." I stuffed it into my mouth and sat down, working my Nikes on.

"So, I heard the cops tracked you down?" Jackie propped her chin on her fist, her eyes darting between the two of us. I looked to Lydia for help and caught her gazing at Dario as if she wanted to spread him across her toast and eat him.

"Yeah." I shoved on the second shoe with a little more force than necessary, and my pinkie toe howled in protest. "It wasn't bad. Just long. Lots of personal questions." That was a bit of an understatement. They all but asked me what positions we screw in. Thank God for Dario's attorney. She jumped in with objections, kept me from saying too much, and ended the interview before I blew a gasket.

I got it. They wanted to find Gwen's killer. They needed to know that I was innocent. Still, the suite's door history told them all they needed, in terms of my involvement.

An old master key was used at 9:19pm.

Gwen's key code was used at 11:02pm.

Someone exited the room at 11:06pm.

My key code was used at 11:15pm.

Dario's code was used a few minutes after that.

Simple freaking breadcrumbs, all backed up by garage and elevator footage. They knew that Dario and I were innocent. What they didn't seem to know was anything about the killer. He had apparently taken the stairwell. Stayed in the blind spots of cameras. Used a master key that had been dormant for four years.

"That one guy was pretty cute. The black cop with the sexy lips?" Jackie stared at me as if I had any earthly idea who she was talking about.

"Not cop," Lydia corrected. "Detective."

"Oooh." Jackie nodded. "Right. Even hotter. Was he there? Did he question you?"

"Uh, no." I looked up at the sound of the front door slamming shut.

"Where are my favorite bitches?"

I dropped my head back and groaned at Rick's voice. Whyyyyy? Why had I wanted to return to normalcy? I could be in a fluffy white Ritz Carlton robe right now, getting my soles massaged as I sipped a mimosa and dozed off poolside in a lounge chair.

Lance's voice chimed into the madness. "Please tell me that's Bell's new Bentley in the driveway."

"It's not!" I called out, then got caught in the kitchen's doorway, hugged by Rick, then Lance, then both of them. I fussed and grouched my way through the hugs, but held each one a moment longer than necessary, and kissed them each on the cheek. "Thanks for bringing the lasagna here."

Lance nodded and reached out a hand to shake Dario's. "You can thank your Mom for that. She practically duct-taped it to me on the way out the door. You going to see them today?"

I nodded, meeting Dario's eyes. "Yeah. That's on the list." I was getting antsy with the need to see them. I had called home yesterday, before Laurent had taken me to the airport, but it hadn't been enough to calm their fears. And it *definitely* hadn't been enough to cure my homesickness. Even though I'd been in Louisiana less than a week, it had felt like a month. I'd narrowly escaped murder, and my parents had watched a news report announcing my death. An in-person visit was in order. Plus, Mom promised me baked macaroni and cheese and had called in sick to work. I wasn't letting those sacrifices go to waste.

"Both of you going there?" Lance looked between us, and I swear to God, this kitchen couldn't get any smaller.

"Yeah." Dario nodded. "We'll head out to Mohave this afternoon."

We. The word seemed to be in giant capital letters, a spotlight dancing across it. WE. WE are going to see her parents. My frown deepened, and he tilted his head as if to suggest we continue the conversation outside, which sounded like a great plan. I stepped to the left and Lance blocked my exit.

"Whoa. We just battled Vegas traffic to see you. Spend a few minutes here. Let us soak up the presence of Bell Hartley."

Dario skirted around the group and headed for the hall. "Take your time. I'll be in the car, whenever you're ready."

I nodded, watched him escape, then was yanked back into the arms of Lance.

"Fuck, girl. This scared the shit out of me," Lance mumbled.

"Yeah, me too." *Me too.*

"Oh my God, pull away now, before they hang up streamers." I plopped down into the passenger seat, the leather warm against the back of my legs, and shut the door.

He shifted into reverse, the car growling as it backed up, then purred into drive. I pulled a baseball cap from my bag and put it on, waving to Meredith, who stepped onto the front porch.

"She's a nice girl. More manageable than the other two."

I smiled at the word *manageable*. With any other friends, I might have been offended, but Lydia and Jackie? *Tolerable* was a more honest way of putting it. "Yeah. She's my favorite. I think she approves of you, too."

Dario turned the corner. "I was thinking I'd drop you off at your parents' house. Give you a chance to spend some time with them. I have some business I can handle while you visit with them."

My nerves, which had begun to knot up each vertebra, relaxed, one stress point gone. My parent's reception of Dario was more likely to be hostile than friendly. That dread, paired with my attempt to explain our relationship ... I readjusted the seat belt across my shoulder. "That would be great."

"How long do you want to stay there? A few hours?"

I glanced at the clock. We'd slept in late. That, paired with the morning sex and Eggo feast—it was already one. "Two hours would be fine. I don't know if I could handle more than that." I grimaced. "I think it's going to be a combination of smothering and inter-rogation."

He reached over, his hand covering mine and giving it a firm squeeze. "I can be there if that will help."

Ha. I laughed and shook my head. "No. The only thing more awkward than discussing our relationship with my parents is for me to do it *with* you." I peeked at him with a wince. "No offense."

He smiled. "None taken. To be honest, I don't have a great track record with fathers."

I thought of Robert Hawk and felt a little queasy, my concerns about my parents so trivial in comparison to Gwen's. The car picked up speed and a delicate breeze softly passed over my face. I had the sudden yearning for my old car, a Mustang convertible. When you put the top down on that, a cyclone of wind was created, conversation impossible unless you wanted to chew hair and scream at each other at the top of your lungs. In that, I could have avoided conversation and used the drive to think over what I was going to say to my parents.

Dario cleared his throat. "Just a reminder, tomorrow ... Gwen's funeral is at one."

"Oh." I hadn't realized, the days running together... I took a deep breath. "I wish I could go with you. Or support you, somehow."

We had discussed this on the plane. It certainly wasn't appropriate for me to be there, and honestly, Dario probably needed the time on his own to mourn. Still, I felt like I was abandoning him.

"If you still want to grab lunch with Meredith, maybe that would be a good time."

"Yeah." I nodded. "Good idea." I needed the time with her. Ever since San Diego, things had moved so quickly, and my heart and head hadn't had time to catch up. I needed to talk through things with a judgment-free third party.

I reached into my bag and pulled out my latest phone. "I'll text her now and see if she's free."

"Just let me know where you'll be eating so we can arrange security."

I opened my mouth. Shut it. Abandoned the text and turned to him. "I don't need security." The words came out calm and controlled, the statement of a sane individual and not one seconds away from opening the convertible's door, Evil Knieveling it into the ditch, and then high-tailing it off into the forest.

Dario's face tightened. "Someone tried to kill you last week."

"And he's dead. Which is why you brought me back. So—"

"I'd rather be safe. Just for a few weeks or a couple of months. Just until we figure out everything about Hawk and track down who he hired to kill you."

He took his eyes off the road and looked over at me. I could see the concern in his eyes, the worry over my safety. I could see it and wasn't sure if I loved or hated it. That's why he was taking me to Mohave. He was *chaperoning* me. I swallowed that immature thought and tried to accept his logic. He was right. It was better to be safe. Still, I hated the idea of security. I thought of someone like Tim and Jim and what it would be like to have them next to me, watching me dip shrimp tempura rolls into soy sauce and wasabi. I thought of them reporting my locations and activities back to Dario, and my vision turned an ugly orange color.

"I don't like the idea of someone tailing me. You have to understand, you've stepped over boundaries at almost every point in our relationship. I can't give you permission to give me security and not expect you to take it too far."

He yanked the car across two lanes of traffic, vibrated over the sleep strips and came to a sudden stop on the shoulder, the seatbelt suddenly tight, pinning me in place. I put a hand out, gripping the dash for support, and looked at him.

He jerked the car into park. "Our relationship needs to change, right now, if that's what you think of me."

I raised a hand, citing his actions as if I'd been keeping score. "Hiring someone to follow me. Sending a hot guy in with fifty grand to see if I was a prostitute. Finding out my phone number without me giving it to you. Turning my phone off without asking me first. Shoving a suite down my throat that I didn't want."

His mouth twitched. "But you're *so* good at taking things down that throat."

I glared at him, and he sobered.

"Okay, yes. I don't trust people, and I don't believe in wasting time. I met you and I couldn't..." He blew out a breath.

"Just stop for a minute." I held up my hand, thinking. I didn't need him to rehash and explain every action. Some of them, when examined under a magnifying glass, made sense. Others didn't. I knew he was different than most men. I understood that a relationship with him wouldn't be easy, and that he was an alpha male in every good—and bad—sense of the word. I was okay with that, but I needed to

126

know that he respected my decisions and opinions. I needed to know that *I* was in control of my life, and that felt like a very questionable concept after I'd let him and Laurent control my every action after Gwen's death.

I looked up to find him waiting, one hand on the steering wheel, a blur of cars in the background, the Vegas skyline barely visible in the dust. "I'll take security. But I can't feel like they are spying on me. I need to have some layer of freedom and privacy."

He looked away from me, studying the road, the cars whizzing past, a lost Styrofoam cup tumbling across the shoulder. I watched his fingers drum on the steering wheel, then he tightened his grip on the wheel, the cords in his forearm bulging.

"Your safety isn't something that I want to compromise on. My team can make sure—"

"Okay." I interrupted him, reaching out and tugging on his shirt, bringing his attention back to me. "But don't go crazy on covering me. Like this moment, right now. You're the only one protecting me. And I'm safe. I don't need a huge protection detail."

His jaw tightened, and I saw frustration weigh down his features. "Fine. But the minute I feel you're unprotected, I'm bringing in more. You have to understand; I just lost Gwen. I just failed her. I can't lose you. Not to some loose end of Hawk's, not to a random stranger on the street, not to a drunk driver on The Strip. And that brings up a second issue."

Great. I fought the urge to sigh. "What's the second issue?"

"Your job. When are you planning on returning to work?"

I shrugged. "I don't know. I haven't had a chance to talk to Rick or Lance about it. I'm assuming they need me back soon. This weekend or next week."

He shook his head. "I can't control the environment there. The entry security protocol is lax. It'd be too easy for someone with talent to get in, get close to you, and hurt you."

My throat closed. "I can't quit my job, Dario."

Out of everything that had happened, this suddenly seemed like the obstacle we couldn't overcome. Quit The House? Leave Rick and Lance? Give up that income? What would be next? College? If he "couldn't control" my job, how would he be able to control UNLV? I felt the swell of hysteria build and looked away, blinking rapidly, trying to control the tears that welled, the lump in my throat growing bigger. I inhaled sharply, a shuddering gasp that didn't give me near enough oxygen.

"Hey." He reached out, and I turned further away, concentrating on the peak of a faraway mountain, trying to collect my thoughts. How had I not seen this coming? How, in all of those empty hours in Louisiana, had I not understood the aftermath of Gwen's death? *Everything has changed now.* He'd said that, and I'd nodded—thinking of the weights that had lifted off of our relationship, not thinking of the chains it had added.

"Bell." His hand wrapped around my forearm, and he tugged, his voice soft and concerned, its gentleness making everything worse.

"Everything's changed." I spoke so softly that I wondered if he heard me. Swallowing hard, I repeated the words, then turned to glare at him. "I'm not giving everything up. Do you understand that? You—"

You aren't worth that. I almost said it but realized the falsity before it materialized. He *was* worth it.

Could I take a hiatus from work? *Yes.*

Could I take classes online? *Probably.*

Could I pause school for a semester considering I wasn't even sure what major I wanted? *Yeah.*

"This is temporary. It won't be like this forever. We'll find systems that work for you. I promise."

I nodded, unwilling to discuss it right now. There was too much to fight about. Security. Work. He hadn't even brought up school, but it was only a matter of time before he did. We were on the way to my parents' house. I couldn't climb up this mountain now.

He studied me, his pupils darting over my features and closing in on my eyes. "Don't appease me, Bell."

I closed my eyes and let out a breath. Opened them back up and gave him my best attempt at a smile. "I'm fine. Let's go before we get slammed from behind by an asshole."

He didn't pull out. He waited for a minute, one so long that it almost stretched into two. He waited for me to say something, but I didn't. I buried my emotions, my fears, my anger. I stuffed it all deep inside me, letting it fester and spoil, and forced my expression to calm, my smile to brighten, my voice to lift. He shifted into drive, and I fiddled with the radio. The car ripped up to speed, and I blared a pop song about kissing boys and spring break. His hand found my knee, and I closed my eyes and fought the urge to vomit.

THE FBI

The Robert Hawk estate was a monstrosity. Twenty thousand square feet full of locked doors, wall safes and the best security money could buy.

A mobile command center squatted on the manicured front lawn, uniforms swarmed the house, and cadaver dogs sniffed the four-acre property for hours without discovery. It took twenty-seven hours and a comparison of the original architectural plans with the current layout to discover the room. Three hundred unaccounted for square feet in between the study and the master suite. The original floorplan had it as a nursery, the door to which was now a solid wall with a hundred-thousand-dollar oil painting hung in its center. They moved the art and found drywall and wainscoting. Searched every seam for a hidden door and finally went Pablo Escobar on the wall, bringing in sledgehammers and splintering through the construction.

It was worth it. Inside, in the cramped, dust-filled space, they found her.

BELL

The greeting was awkward. Dario walked me up the steps, introduced himself and extended his hand. Dad stared at it as if it was diseased. Mom invited Dario to come inside. I declined on his behalf, then practically pushed him down the front stairs, giving him an apologetic kiss before I scampered back inside.

That was five minutes ago, and Dad *still* stood in the doorway, one hand on the frame, and peered through the screen door as if it was a Magic Eye puzzle.

"Stop staring, Dad."

He sniffed. "Fancy car he's got. What'd that put him back?"

My mom glared at him from her spot by the stove. "You haven't seen your daughter in a week, and you're interested in the man's car? Get in here."

He didn't move. "Bell's not going anywhere. I think he's talking to himself."

I looked past him, watching as Dario slowly reversed, his mouth moving. "He's on the phone, Dad. It's called Bluetooth. The car has a microphone that connects to his cell phone."

Mom let out an exasperated huff. "He knows what Bluetooth is, Bell. He's just being ornery. Mike, are you gonna eat or gawk? Go wash your hands."

I popped ice from the trays and filled up the glasses with water, watching as Dad slowly ambled up to the sink, his hip nudging me to the side as he took over, working the bar of soap over his hands. He dried them off on the towel, and I passed him his water, giving him a kiss on the cheek.

Mom set down the plates, and I settled in at my seat. Mother said grace, and I barely had time to grab a napkin before Dad started in on me.

"So... the news first told us that you were dead. But actually..." He jabbed a thumb in the direction that Dario had been. "It was this guy's *wife* who died. And now he's driving you over here. And called us and talked to us about you without telling us anything at all."

I looked to Mom for help, but she said nothing, her eyebrows rising in their own request for an explanation. I stuck in a giant forkful of mac and cheese and took my dear sweet time chewing it.

He waited, his own plate ignored. Mom waited, her hands clasped together as if still in prayer. Even Rascal, sitting beside me, his tongue lolling out one side of his mouth, let out a whine that seemed to say *confess everything, you heathen.*

So, I did. I took a deep breath, swallowed the chunk of cheesy goodness, and started at the beginning, skipping over my sexy times with Ian, my slutty texts, and every thrust, moan and naked moment.

I confessed it all and waited for judgment.

THE FBI

The girl drank, guzzling back the Gatorade, her throat flexing, eyes closing, both hands cupped around the bottle as if it were gold. Her name was Katy Dunning. Her boyfriend had reported her missing three months ago. She'd come to Vegas for a bachelorette weekend and never came home. Vegas PD hadn't thought much about it, and her face hadn't been in Hawk's file of potential victims. Agent King watched the girl and wondered how many other tourist abductions they'd missed.

She finished the Gatorade and set it carefully down on the table, her swollen wrists catching his eye. They'd found her handcuffed to a concrete wall, her arms stretched out to either side, her legs weak from standing. She'd burst into tears at the sight of them. Now, she blinked and a fresh volley ran down her cheeks.

Agent King waited a beat before speaking. "If you can start at the beginning, we need to know as many details as you can remember."

She nodded, her fingers carefully passing over an open cut on her wrist, the damage caused by the cuffs. He noticed and motioned to the woman next to him, who rose to fetch a paramedic.

"I was in the bathroom of 44th Broad. Washing my hands at the sink. Someone came up behind me and put something over my eyes, and my mouth. I struggled, I tried to fight, but everything just … went out of me. I couldn't move, I forgot what I was doing. I got so heavy..." She looked down at the bottle. "Can I have more Gatorade, please? I'm really thirsty."

He nodded. "Sure. We'll get you some more. Please keep going."

She shrugged. "Then I woke up and I was chained up. I struggled, but couldn't get loose."

He made a notation on his pad of paper. "And you've been in that room ever since? He didn't move you at all?"

She looked up sharply, a bit of greasy blonde hair falling out from behind her ear. "Oh, no. This was before. This was at the first place. The warehouse."

The door of the trailer swung open, and the paramedic stepped in, followed by the female agent. Agent King held up a hand, signaling them to wait. "A warehouse?" He watched her closely, seeing her eyes jump from him to the paramedic.

She nodded. "Yeah. A big one. You know. Where all the other girls are."

The female agent locked eyes with him, the tension in the room spiking. "Katy, we need you to tell us everything you can about the warehouse and as quickly as possible."

SEVENTEEN

BELL

I dipped the bowl into the soapy water and heard the living room television turn on. The sponge was slimy, and I added more soap to it, rubbing the stiff side over the ceramic.

"Your dad is just going to need some time to adjust to things," Mom spoke quietly, turning on the faucet to drown out our conversation. "He's never liked your boyfriends, you know that."

She was right. Even sweet, perfect Elliot. He had picked me up for our first date, and Dad had slunk into their bedroom and hadn't talked to me for three days.

Mom continued. "Plus, Dario is much more *man* than you've ever dated. That's hard for your father, looking up at a man bigger than him. He can't intimidate Dario, and—this last week—he's felt helpless in terms of reaching or protecting you."

"I know." I passed her the bowl and reached for another. "I just wanted one part of this to go smoothly. I was hoping this would be it."

She pulled the dirty bowl from my hands and set it in the sink, turning me to face her. I looked up into her face and noticed, for the first time in years, that she was getting old. She had new bags under her light brown eyes. Her hair, which she'd dyed blonde for as long as I'd lived, was streaked with silver. She wasn't that old. Fifty-three. Too young to be looking at me with such old eyes.

"What's different about him?"

It was a steep question, one that would take a week to answer. I met her eyes and gave the best answer I could. "Everything."

It was true. Everything was different about him. Some of it I didn't want, some of it I loved. But everything about him—the issues, the sincerity, the passion, the love ... it was all authentic. I trusted him. That was the biggest thing about him. I lost my breath when he looked at me. I swooned when he reached for me. I loved him, even if I didn't fully understand it. Even when I hated him.

She pulled me into her soft chest and wrapped her arms around me. I melted into the embrace. She turned her head, her lips against my ear, and spoke quietly. "We just want you to be happy. And safe. We worry, with everything that has happened with him, that he's putting you in danger."

I pulled away and kissed her cheek. "That's all done, Mom. I promise. And he's still wanting to drown me in security. So, don't worry. I'm safe."

"Your heart, too?" She smiled, but I heard the concern in her voice.

I smiled back. "My heart too."

⊡

THE ONLY

Robert's arrest changed everything. She had read the news ticker and headed for The Majestic. Used her access codes to get into the executive garage and behind the wheel of an SUV. By the time she'd started the engine, his shooting was all over the radio.

Men like Robert weren't supposed to die. She had failed. She had destroyed everything. For him to be arrested, and then killed? Shot down like a common man?

It had sent her psyche spiraling in an entirely different direction: rage.

She shifted into drive and headed to the one place he loved.

The warehouse was at the center of a gated complex that spanned almost two hundred acres. The gate surrounding it was ten feet high, with an electric wire running along its top edge, every foot monitored by motion detectors and cameras. Its location had been carefully chosen, in the middle of the desert, a stealth approach impossible. Escape, should someone make it over the fence and past the electric current, would involve a lengthy hike through the unforgiving desert.

In the twelve years since the warehouse's creation, only one girl had attempted escape. She'd made it to the fence. Burned and shuddered through the electric wires. Fallen the ten feet to the desert rock and broken an arm and wrist. Stumbled about eighty yards before Hawk's gun had caught her, his crosshairs aimed at her legs.

She was hung in the middle of the warehouse as a warning. Her body had swelled in the Vegas heat. Flesh rotted. Blood collected in her lower limbs and her feet turned black. The smell grew, permeating through every cell, a constant reminder of the display. Flies appeared, and the girls took to facing the back walls of their prisons.

After a few weeks, the smell faded, but the body remained. Hope withered and no one else tried to escape. It didn't matter. Now that Hawk was dead, they'd all die anyway. The only question was how and when.

Claudia pulled open the cell door and glanced over the empty space, one that reeked of urine and feces. Pulling her hair into a high ponytail, she donned a mask, then wheeled the pressure washer into the center of the room, parking it to the side of the large drain hole. The drain was more of a grate, with slats large enough to accommodate bits of body, if Hawk got creative with his disposal. Typically, it was used for circumstances like this. The drain carried the remains into a septic tank that sat underneath the warehouse, one large enough to hold another two decades worth of filth. A useless arrangement, given Hawk's sudden absence. There would soon be no need for disposals. No need for the burning pit or the instruments, the carefully orchestrated entertainment for their pets, or the training. The leader was gone and continuing the activities without him seemed pointless.

But before she blew this warehouse to pieces, it would host two final guests. Two guests that would require every bit of training she had ever received from him. Two guests that would receive the full range of the Robert Hawk brutality. It was only right, seeing as they were responsible for his death.

She switched on the pressure washer, the loud roar of the engine filling the space. Pointing the sprayer at a splash of blood on the wall, she squeezed the nozzle, a combination of bleach and water shooting out of it. Focusing on the streak of crimson, her fury mounting, she began to prep the cell for their arrival.

DARIO

Dario leaned against the car, the nozzle in the tank, and waited for it to fill. Holding the phone to his ear, he listened to the FBI agent.

"We're still questioning her, trying to get as many details as possible that will help us pinpoint a location. But just from scanning through Hawk's tax registrations, we have five or six possibilities. The man owns more property than God."

Dario watched as a pickup truck pulled in, the diesel engine loud as it stopped next to him. He turned his head, shielding the receiver with his hand. "If he was doing anything questionable, he wouldn't have it under his own name. He's the king of shell corporations. You're going to have to get a forensic accountant to dig deep. Look for something big, and something close by. The man hates to fly, so it'd be something in driving distance."

Hated. The man *hated* to fly. It was so odd, talking about him in the past tense. It seemed false—his larger than life adversary gone too easily.

The FBI agent's voice crackled through the cell. "We're on it. I don't have to explain to you that this is our top priority. Especially with the chance that some of these girls are still alive."

He was almost glad Gwen wasn't here to see this. They had never discussed the rumors that swirled around her father. He'd brought it up once, and she'd stopped him quickly, her face tightening into a stiff glare that he'd never seen before. She'd insisted on his innocence, and he'd let the matter go. Finding whatever horrors existed in this warehouse would have broken her and destroyed whatever remaining faith she had left in her image of family.

Ending the call, he hung up the gas nozzle and got into the car, anxious to get back to Bell.

BELL

Dario was quiet, which suited me. He'd updated me on the girl they'd found in Hawk's house. Her story and the mental image of a warehouse full of prisoners had my mind working overtime. I'd thought Gwen's shooting had been a terrible way to die. Now, I was suddenly reminded of all of the more gruesome ways to go.

We entered Mohave, which is to say that we passed the Dairy Queen and the 35 MPH sign carefully hidden behind an enthusiastic shrub that law enforcement like to pour fertilizer on in their spare time. I tapped Dario's arm. "Slow down. This car sticks out like a sore thumb."

He obeyed, surprising me when he put on his blinker and turned into Becky's Diner.

"What are we doing?"

He pulled down a busy row and idled before an empty spot. "I want to take my girl on a date. I know you had an early dinner, but are you up for dessert?"

I squinted at the diner and fought back my smile. "At Becky's Diner?"

He managed to look hurt. "What? Not fancy enough for you?" He twisted in his seat, looking up and down the quiet street. "I hate to break your heart, but I'm not sure what other options we have."

"Becky's is fine. I'm just not sure you want to pick this night of the week to eat here."

He pulled into the spot and turned off the ignition. "Meaning what?"

I grinned and cracked open the door. "You'll see."

In Vegas, you gamble. In Louisiana, you eat crawfish. In Mohave, you play trivia at Becky's on Monday night. Other than fucking, racing dune buggies, and chasing kids ... there's not much else to do. It'd been two years since I last stepped foot in Becky's, but I pushed open the door, and it was exactly the same.

The scents of beer, grease, and perfume-laced body odor.

A collective din of noise, voices and clattering utensils against dishes.

Babies with unwiped drool waving food-covered hands in the air.

A floor that was slightly sticky underfoot.

Tables crowded, ringed with t-shirts, big hair, and baseball caps.

We stopped in the doorway and Brenda freakin' Bishop was the first one to see me.

"Bell Hartley, is that *you?*" She jostled to her feet, her pregnant belly swinging, and held out her arms.

I hugged her and waved to the others at her table. "Hey Brenda. Jay. Jimbo. Annette."

They nodded, knocked around their chairs in an attempt to make room for us, then gave up.

"Who's your friend?" Annette Torres gazed up at Dario with fascination, a look that earned her a scowl from her husband.

I pushed Dario forward, catching sight of an open table near the back. "This is Dario. We're gonna grab that table before it's taken. Good luck, guys."

Between the door and the table, we were stopped twice more. Two more introductions of Dario, two more hugs. By the time we made it to the empty two-top, I was reminded why I confined my Mohave visits to my parent's small scrap of dirt.

"Popular girl." Dario picked up a menu.

"Not really. But you're gossip gold, so everyone's going to want to have something to share." I leaned forward and gently tugged the menu out of his hand. "On trivia night, the normal menu's dead. The only thing they have is burgers. With cheese or without. With fries or not."

"Trivia night?"

As if on cue, the kitchen door swung open and a three-hundred-pound bowling ball of a man, dipped in gold eyeshadow, daisy-print coveralls and bright yellow cowboy boots, waltzed into the room. A general cheer went up, and Dario's mouth twitched.

"Who is that, exactly?"

I smiled and lifted my hand, waving to Sally, the bartender. "Oh, that's Becky."

"*That's* Becky?" His grin widened, and I fought the urge to kiss it.

Becky dragged his stool to the front of the restaurant and straddled it, withdrawing a bedazzled microphone out of his front bib pocket. I reached into the ceramic pot in the center of the table and pulled out an answer form and tiny pencil.

"Trivia night with Becky." Dario read out the title on the answer form and watched as I carefully wrote the date on top of the answer sheet. "Well, this should be interesting."

Interesting? I smiled to myself. He had no idea.

EIGHTEEN

"We need a name." I stared at the blank line at the top of the form, my mind void of creative spark.

"Just put Bell and Dario."

I frowned at him. "It needs to be something else. Something..."

Something ... something that didn't scream *Bell Hartley is back in town and in a relationship* in giant capital letters. Not that I was ashamed of it. But prancing around with the guy who cut John and Johnny's balls off was probably ...not a good idea. This was Mohave, after all. Gossip spread quickly, and we already had enough of it buzzing around the room as it is. Dario's foot bumped mine as he settled into his seat, and I stared at the blank line.

Becky bellowed into the microphone, the feedback screeching through the room. "Trivia starts in five minutes, folks! Put your food orders in and get your cobwebs cleaned outta those skulls! Tonight's prize is a $25 gift card to Kevin's Guns and a free appetizer!"

Dario snorted and I shot him a glare.

"Come on. Think of something."

"What about The Gamblers?" he suggested.

I made a face and he laughed.

"What? We are risk-takers. Everything about us has been a risk so far."

A risk we, and others, have paid for. I shook my head. "It's too obvious."

"The Risk-Takers?"

I curled up my nose. "Sounds like an eighties band."

I scratched the back of my hand. "What about a poker term? Or—"

"Double Down," he suggested.

It wasn't terrible, though it did sound a little dude ranchy. Still, the origins behind the title raised my interests and I met his gaze. "Why Double Down?"

He leaned forward. "It fits us. You could have given up when Gwen died. Or kept the stakes the same. But you didn't. I didn't. We risked more. Raised the stakes. Emotionally, went in deeper. At least, I did."

"Me too." I looked down at the page. Doubling down was a black-jack term. It's when you had a risky hand that had the potential to be strong, or the potential to be disastrous. Instead of riding the hand out, you double your bet. And in doing so, you wager every-thing on the next card. That card determines your outcome—and is statistically more likely to tank your hand than win it.

It *did* fit us. On paper, we were a losing hand. Yet we'd both stayed in and, as he said, risked more.

I wrote Double Down on the line, then looked back up on him. "That's good."

"You like it?"

I nodded, and when he tugged on my hand, pulling me in for a kiss, I didn't fight it.

DARIO

She was intoxicating. When she laughed, it pulled at something inside of him, each instance unraveling one more loose thread that held onto his pain. When she looked at him, the way she was right now, her gaze drifting over his lips, her eyes heavy with need, it lit a fire in him in a way no one had ever done. He reached over and picked up her hand. Turned the delicate wrist over and pressed a kiss against it. She curled her fingers around his jaw and all he wanted was a lifetime with her. Mornings in bed. Calls from her in the middle of his day. Her body curled against his at night. Her, in an evening gown, in Paris. Sandy and sunburnt in Exuma. Pregnant and glowing in a doctor's office.

It was endearing, how competitive she was. It had been a surprising trait to encounter. Tiny fangs and claws had sprung out, her focus intense on winning a useless gift card and free appetizer they would never use. And they *weren't* going to win. Whoever wrote these questions was a sadist, evidenced in point by the current query.

"You're useless." She tapped the tip of the pencil on the page, trying to think of an answer for the question Becky had just asked. "Come on. THINK."

He shook his head. "I told you. I don't know anything about Madonna."

"Shit."

She put her head in her hands and stared down at the page. "Her first husband. I know this. It's not Guy Ritchie. There's no way she didn't get married until then."

She peered at him as if he was deliberately withholding the information. "Come on. Think of anyone she dated in the eighties."

He laughed. "I'm thirty-seven, Bell. I barely knew what marriage was in the eighties. And I definitely wasn't paying attention to Madonna."

And shit, in Louisiana? His dad had played Hank Williams, Jr and creole music. If someone had put Madonna on the juke box, they would have gotten thrown out of the bar.

She slumped in the seat and picked up her soda. "We're going to lose."

Her gaze connected with his, and he smiled. Her dejection mellowed, her lips turning up at the ends, and that look, the one that made his dick stand on end, came back to her eyes.

"Oh... yoo hoo!" The man with the gold eyeshadow tapped the microphone. "Put those pencils down, because it's time for the next question and this one is a show-stopper."

Dario nodded for the exit. "Let's get out of here."

She lifted one adorable shoulder in a shrug. "It's probably best. We don't want to embarrass these guys with our awesome score."

"Such a giver."

She laughed. "You got cash?"

Dario nodded, sitting forward and pulling his wallet out of his back pocket. Thumbing through the bills, he grabbed a few and tossed them on the table. He stood and her hand found his, tugging slightly as she led the way out of the restaurant.

She curled against the seat, facing him, her dark hair twisted up into a messy ponytail. From the radio, Andrea Bocelli softly crooned, the rich notes floating over the car's interior and out into the night.

"Where are we going?" she asked.

He glanced over at her. "I thought I'd leave that up to you. Do you want to go back to your house?"

He dreaded the thought. It had been pure bedlam in that house. Noise until three in the morning, then someone up and banging around at seven. The door seemed to never stop, visitors dropping by unannounced, security an absolute nightmare. Before staying there, he had wanted her to have her own place. After staying there, it was no longer up for discussion. She needed a secure home, one where he could properly protect her. If she wanted her independence, if she wanted to bring all of those crazy women and hecticness with her, and live separately from him—fine. But it needed to be behind a gate, with cameras and alarms and a shower that didn't run cold and could accommodate a grown man without molesting him with the curtain.

She shook her head and he breathed a sigh of relief. "I need a full night's sleep. In a bed big enough to hold both of us." She grinned at him and he reached over, cupping her knee, unable to resist the urge to touch her.

Yes, he needed her in bed. Loud. Moaning. Bent over. Thrusting back. Naked. Panting. Coming apart. His mouth against her slick mound. His tongue dipping inside, running along her slit, lightly feasting on her clit. Her thighs trembling. Mouth opening. Body clenching. He'd move up her body, then. Settle between her legs, her muscles still twitching, pulsing. Hot and wet. He'd push inside, feel her tighten, her nails clawing along his chest, her eyes opening, body reawakening. He'd never had a woman so responsive, so engaged. When she was touched, she bloomed. When he fucked her, she was a rabid animal. When he made love to her, she melted.

His hand tightened, sliding up her thigh, his fingers passing over the smooth skin, itching to be past the frustrating fabric of her shorts and inside her heat. She exhaled, a whimper of invitation in the tone. He could make her come right now. Softly strum her clit through her panties. Lean back that seat. Open up those legs. She could brace her feet on the dash. Arch into his hand. He could slip in a finger, crook it against her g-spot, and she'd come undone.

He saw an exit and didn't hesitate, the Bentley taking the change with ease, the off-ramp slightly bumpy as they pulled off the highway and onto a side road, coasting down the dark lane, under tree cover, and pulling off to the side.

She didn't ask questions. She didn't hesitate. She popped the button on her shorts, pulled them down the length of her legs, and reclined back, opening her thighs to him, her yellow panties almost glowing in the dark. He cut off the lights and reached for her, his need only eclipsed by his awe.

God, she was perfect, in absolutely every way.

BELL

I lay on his chest, the expensive sheets cool along my back, his heartbeat thudding against my ear. My body twitched, an after-effect of the orgasm, and I closed my eyes, enjoying the sensation. Doubts wormed their way along my subconscious, interrupting my slumber, and I attempted to push them away. I didn't deserve this. Him. This expensive suite, the butler service, the view. It all felt too perfect, too different, like I was Cinderella and—any moment—the clock would hit midnight.

His hand ran along my back. "Don't give up on me, on us."

It was annoying, how the man seemed to read my mind. Not that I was giving up on him, or on us. But my thoughts were colliding, my doubts rising and bringing my anxiety along with it.

I rolled over and stared up at the ceiling. "I feel as if everything's about to fall apart again."

"It's not. Besides, we're through the worst of it. Hawk is gone. He can't touch us anymore."

I turned to him, repositioning so that I was on my side, face to face with him. I reached out, my fingers gently tracing over his features. "*Are* we through the worst of it? You make it sound like it's over. Like people aren't dead."

Dead. It sounded like a curse word, and I wanted to take it back the moment it left my lips. I saw the impact when it hit Dario, the flinch of his features, the tightness of that mouth, the darkness of his eyes.

"Let me carry that guilt. It wasn't you. It was me."

"No."

I struggled to prop myself up on one elbow, to gain some sort of stance. I'd heard the tone of those words before, recognized the pain in his features, the anguish in his eyes. My mother felt that guilt because I'd needed to work and help them cover the bills. Working at the barn had led to my rape. My mother carried that guilt because she'd been at the diner, and not able to pick me up, not able to be there when John had driven by and seen the barn light on. My father had felt that guilt when he'd been too drunk to be taken seriously, when his reputation with the Mohave police department overshadowed his teenage daughter's statement. *I* had felt that guilt, for not saying no clearly enough. For being there. For not running. For every time I'd let Johnny's eyes slide over me without glaring back.

Our guilt had been ill-placed, and it had almost broken our family. I couldn't bear to see it break us. But I also didn't know what to say. Because unlike my parents—Dario and I *were* to blame. Hawk had been the dynamite, but we had lit the fuse.

"Just love me through the cracks." His voice was gruff, and when he pulled me to him, I flexed into the warmth of his chest.

"You're the only thing holding me together, Bell. Just tell me you won't give up on me." He kissed my forehead, then my cheeks, the brush of his lips tender, then almost desperate. *Dario needed me.* Me. In this moment, he wasn't the arrogant alpha male I knew. He wasn't the King of Vegas. He was stripped bare of anything outside of this room, and he was mine. *Needed to be mine.* And I would never give up on him. *Never.*

I lifted my mouth to his. "I won't give up on us, Dario. I love you."

His mouth pressed against mine and I tasted, in the moment before he returned the words, his pain.

He was broken. Like me.

Love me through the cracks.

I would. I did. There was no way I could walk away now.

NINETEEN

BELL

I woke up to SILENCE. Cool room, warm bed, the sight of Dario shaving at the sink. His back muscles were insane, rivulets of dips and curves that had my fingers itching to pull back the sheets and explore. He wore black boxer briefs, the underwear's package open on the bed. I sat up, holding the fluffy white blanket against my bare chest, and eyed the gold bag at the entrance to the bathroom.

"Good morning."

He turned at the words, half of his face smooth, a razor in hand. It was a good look. I pulled the blanket back and slid off the bed, walking toward him.

"That's a sight I could become addicted to." He reached for me, pulling me against him and I raised to my toes, kissing him.

I tugged the razor from his hand. "Let me finish."

His hands settled on my bare hips, slid upward to my waist, and he lifted me up, setting me on the marble surface, a wicked gleam in his dark brown eyes. The counter was cold against my ass, and when he pushed my knees open and moved closer, the feel of air between my legs felt deliciously sexual.

I admired him from this new angle. Still gorgeous. Still ruggedly wild and untamable, even with white foam over half his face. I lifted the razor and pressed the blade of it against his cheekbone.

"Ever done this before?" he asked.

I met his eyes. "No. So be still."

A smile ghosted across his lips. I held his chin still with one hand and dragged the razor down, a path cut between the white.

"You're beautiful when you concentrate."

I smiled and pulled away, leaning to the right and twisting the handle of the sink. Water gushed, and I rinsed the blade underneath it, then returned to his face. I was halfway along his jaw when his hand brushed over my breast.

Pausing, I met his eyes, which held mine. "You're not behaving."

"Your nakedness is distracting me." His palm was warm, his fingers gentle, and he closed his hand softly around my breast, my skin awakening under the contact. I let out a breath and finished the razor's path.

Lifting it from his jaw, I leaned right to rinse the blade, and almost came apart when he tugged softly on my nipple.

"Dario..."

I sat back in place, focusing on his cheek, starting a short stroke down his face. His second hand joined the game, tickling the top of my free nipple, and my knees parted a smidge out of reflex.

I struggled to control my breath and carefully moved the blade across a fresh patch of skin. His eyes met mine, and he reached up, gently swiping the tips of his fingers from my lips ... all the way down the center of my body ... down to my clit.

I lifted the razor from his face before I nicked it. "You're going to make my pussy drip all over this counter if you don't stop."

It was a sentence that unleashed a beast. The razor flew aside, his arms wrapped around my waist, and I was off the counter and against his chest, his hands on my ass, carrying me easily, my legs wrapping around him, our mouths colliding in a hot tangled mess of passion. Shaving cream smeared under my fingers, I tasted it in our kiss, his body still warm from the shower, a landscape of slick muscles against my skin.

We fell onto the bed, and I yanked at his underwear. A half breath later, he was inside me. *God. Fuck. Yes.*

Meredith and I had eaten at Transit a dozen times before. She got the rainbow roll. I liked surf 'n' turf. We'd flirt with the sushi guy and sit at the bar. If we were chatty, we'd get edamame and split some tempura.

It'd been a few weeks since we'd had lunch together, but in that time, everything had changed. "I'm sorry about the excessive security measures," I say leaning forward, making eye contact with her and trying to ignore the fact that two of the six other tables in the restaurant were filled with Dario's men. Big guys, each with a visible gun on their hips. One had a badge. Two had driven us here and now stood watch outside the restaurant.

It was ridiculous. Major overkill. He took my insistence at a light security team and tossed it out the window. And why? We went to Mohave last night without a lick of security. Sat in a crowd at Becky's within a team of armed guards. Managed to feel normal and lived through the night without a single instance of trouble. This wasn't necessary.

"It's a man thing," Meredith explained. "He thinks he can protect you better than anyone else." She lifted one shoulder in a shrug. "Whether it makes sense or not." She wrapped her hands around her tea and inhaled the steam from it. "Just deal with it. Give him a couple of weeks, he'll relax a little. The man's been through a lot."

"Yeah." I thought of him dressing for the funeral. The solemn way he had knotted his tie. The long moment when he had studied his watch before putting it on.

"What?" She nudged me with her foot. "What does that look mean?"

"I don't know."

"Bullshit." She took a sip of tea, then placed the cup down. "What's bothering you?"

"It's just…" I sighed. "I feel terrible even saying it. I—he—he misses her." I looked up from the table. "Does it make me a terrible person to be jealous of that?"

"It makes you normal." She pulled a pair of chopsticks from the wrapper and broke them apart. "Have you talked to him about it?"

"No." I shook my head. "I couldn't even—I mean, I don't want him to feel like he needs to hide that. He should miss her. It just makes me feel insecure in our own relationship. One, because they have— had—such a long history, and so many memories and this hard bedrock of friendship. And two, because it's my fault, or our relationship's fault, that she's gone. So I worry that every time he's hurting over her death, or thinks of her—"

"That he's going to begrudge you for it." She put the pieces together too quickly, a reaction that validated my concerns.

I nodded, sitting back as they delivered our rolls. "Yeah."

"I think…" She plucked an end piece from her roll and popped it in her mouth, leaving me hanging as she slowly chewed the enormous

153

piece. By the time she swallowed, I was ready to stab her with a chopstick.

She cleared her throat. "I think you have to get over it. *All* of it. Stop feeling sorry for yourself. Stop comparing your relationship to his with Gwen. Stop beating yourself up and expecting him to blame you for something that he is just as guilty—NO." She waved a sticky pair of chopsticks in the air between us. "*Fuck* that. Neither of you are to blame for it, but he's a grown ass man. He knew the risks a hell of a lot more than you did. And if he wants to dwell on his own guilt, fine. But you need to pull your head out of the mess on this one. I know you beat yourself up every day in Louisiana over it, but it's time to stop that shit."

I couldn't help but smile at the stern look she gave me, the effectiveness of it hampered slightly by the smear of wasabi along her bottom lip. "Okay," I conceded.

"Don't just blow smoke up my ass," she warned.

"I'm not." I lifted up my hands in surrender. "I promise."

"Good." She glanced around the restaurant and lifted one brow. "Now, are there any rules about dating the help? 'Cause you *know* I've got a weakness for men in uniform."

I smiled at her and wondered how, with everything going on, I would make it without her.

DARIO

Outside of the church, the lines circled the block. He walked down the street toward the church, nodding at the faces, each one somber, some avoiding his eyes. The rumors had already started. Whispers of his infidelity, of his mistress, the circumstances of

Gwen's death... they were too juicy to ignore, and they'd spread like a virus through the city.

How many of them were here out of love for her, and how many were here out of curiosity? It was impossible to know. He climbed the steps and nodded to the usher, who swung open the door with a respectful nod.

"Mr. Capece."

"Thank you." Dario stepped into the cool interior of the church, his eyes adjusting to the dim lighting. "How long do I have?"

"They will begin seating in twenty minutes, sir. If you need more time, please just let us know."

Dario nodded. Moving through the entranceway, he pushed on the heavy double door and entered the main hall of the church. Before him, at the end of a flower-lined aisle, sunlight streaming through stained glass windows, lay the casket. He took a deep, shuddering breath, and started down the aisle.

They'd been married in this church. He'd stood where the foot of the casket now was, and watched as she walked down the aisle. She'd smirked at him, amused by all of the pomp and circumstance. The two of them had been the only ones in the crowded church to know the truth—that their marriage was a sham, their love a façade, but their vows ... at least the ones they had said ... those had been meant.

In sickness and in health.

Till death do us part.

He slowly climbed the steps and stopped at the open casket, looking down at her. His throat tightened and he reached out, gripping the edge of the mahogany. His vision blurred and he swallowed hard, fighting to maintain composure.

"I'm so sorry," he whispered. "You begged me to stay and I just—"

His words broke off and he searched her face, so perfect, so serene. She looked untouched, her hair artfully arranged to hide the exit wound, her makeup simple and elegant. He thought of her in the shower, the way she had clung to him, her pride abandoned, her desperation coating every plea.

She had left that shower and gone to talk to Bell. What had she planned to say? What would have been that outcome? Where had her mind been?

He knew how she had looked, in that last glance she gave him before she left. Disappointed. Hurt. Thirteen years together, and *that* had been their final moment. It broke his heart.

"Oh, Gwen." He lowered his head and closed his eyes, fighting to hold onto a memory, a good memory, of the two of them. "I miss you so much. I hope, wherever you are, that you are at peace." He tried to feel her presence, tried to connect with the perfect and silent body before him, but all he felt was emptiness. Loneliness.

She had been, for a third of his life, his partner. His best friend. His confidante. His sounding board. She had been the first person he saw each morning, and the first number he dialed when something happened.

And now, she was gone.

He tried to pick up her hand, his chest constricting at the stiff set of it. Releasing the hand, he attempted to compose himself. Looking up to the arched ceilings, angels painted along their curves, he told her how much he loved her. He begged her for her forgiveness, and he said the first of a lifetime of goodbyes.

Behind him, the doors to the inner church creaked open, a thin man in a robe entering. "Mr. Capece, would you like more time?"

He shook his head tightly, struggling to tamper his emotions, his façade of composure settling into place. "No. You can begin to bring them in. Thank you."

Turning, he bent over and gave her forehead one final kiss, hating that she no longer smelled like his Gwen. Hating her father for stealing her life, her innocence, her chance at a real future of her own choosing. Hating that ... his throat tightened. He hated that this lonely cold moment was their goodbye.

She had deserved better.

TWENTY

The weight of the funeral was washed away by the open air in the Lamborghini. He tossed Bell the keys, and she drove. Her hesitancy was cute, her exit out of The Majestic's parking garage cautious, the engine over-revving as she shifted into second. But once she got the hang of the gears, her confidence grew to a level that was impressive. She wove around slower traffic, the car responding to her cues, her smile widening with each passing minute. Her beauty was mesmerizing, and he relaxed in the passenger seat, stealing glances at her as she focused on the road.

"This exit."

He pointed and she downshifted. The top was down, the wind whipping her hair, and he was glad he'd left the security back at the hotel, opting to take the convertible instead of the Rolls. They needed this, the time between just the two of them, the normality. They were a man and a woman, house-hunting. Utterly normal. Squint past the exorbitant luxuries and recent dangers, and they could be any other new couple. Maybe, like any other new relationship, they could survive this stage and move on to the next.

"Right or left?" she asked.

"Left, then your first right."

She took her eyes off the road and gave him a quick smile, and it was a brief glimpse of the future. Her tan skin glowing against the neon orange of the Lambo. Her sunglasses perched on the top of her head. Her smile loose and relaxed. Once they moved in, he'd give her a housewarming present and fill one slot in its garage with this car.

"Is the Realtor meeting us there?"

He nodded, checking his phone. His assistant had contacted the listing agents directly, setting up the appointments. They had three houses ahead of them, with three different realtors. He checked his watch. "We're going to be a little early. Feel free to slow down a little."

She snorted, and it was so different from Gwen's reserved polish that he had to take a moment, the grief warring with the love in his heart.

"So, no murals," Dario said, opening the car door and getting in.

"It wasn't so much the murals as what was *on* the murals." She sucked the red straw loudly, her cheeks hollowing from the effort. "I mean, I don't want to look at painted grapevines all day. If it was something cool, like graffiti or abstract art, then maybe..." She paused, then shook her head. "Nah. No murals."

Dario took a sip from his Slurpee, the cherry flavor bringing him back to middle school afternoons and cleaning windshields for cash. He mentioned it to Bell, and she smiled, settling into the passenger side.

"I bet we would have gotten along, had we both grown up at the same time. Two poor kids, working crap jobs for money." Her smile wilted a little, and he spoke quickly, before she walked too far down memory lane.

"I wouldn't have been your friend."

She frowned at him, twisting in the car seat. "Why not?"

"I would have fallen in love with you. Probably made a complete fool of myself and caused you to run in the other direction."

She smiled, and her teeth were faintly stained in an adorable shade of blueberry. She leaned forward and lowered her voice conspiratorially. "I hate to break it to you, but you did make a fool of yourself with me."

He frowned. "I only remember studly acts of valor and coolness."

She increased the volume of her whisper. "Nobody cool says 'coolness' anymore."

She reached out and poked him, and he couldn't stop himself from trapping her hand and pulling her into him. His mouth covered hers, a kiss filled with cold and sugar. Her hand fumbled, reaching out and grabbing his shirt, her mouth pressing harder as she surged forward, across the seat, her need overtaking her.

"I love you." She murmured the words in between kisses, her focus on his lips, the gas station fading into the background as their contact heated up.

"I love you too."

And he did, so much it scared him.

THE FBI

They found the warehouse in a shell corporation that was linked back to Hawk in a complicated tier of paperwork. If they hadn't known what to look for, if Dario hadn't told them of the ways that Hawk creatively structured entities, they could have missed it.

"Move in silently. We can't run this again if we fuck it up." Agent King nodded at the other men, his gaze drifting over the group, many of who he'd worked with for decades. They were older than most in the Bureau, but that was the way he liked it. They wouldn't get trigger happy and shoot the wrong person, or express an opinion when he gave an order.

He lowered his sunglasses and hunched over, passing quietly through the grass and toward the large aluminum building, one big enough to hold a thousand women, though Katy Dunning's statement indicated the number was closer to eight. Eight women, kept away from their families. Eight women, tortured and imprisoned. Eight women who probably hadn't had food or possibly water since Hawk's death. Eight women who could be moments from rescue.

Tightening his hold on his weapon, he quickened his pace, his eyes darting across the building's exterior, searching for movement.

Eight women. Eight lives that were about to be saved.

TWENTY-ONE

BELL

The second house was massive, the sort where Dario could scream his lungs off in one corner, and I wouldn't hear a peep from the other. We parked beside the Realtor's minivan and I eyed the white stucco home. It was beautiful, topped with red tile roofs, and dotted with arched windows, flowering planters, and surrounded by palm trees.

Dario turned off the car and I could hear the sound of a fountain gurgling.

"It feels so peaceful."

Dario pointed to a tree-lined hill that ran along the side of the property. "Don't be fooled. That berm was built to hide the highway. Jog through those trees and you'll be smelling exhaust and weaving across six lanes of traffic."

I tilted my head and realized, barely audible over the fountain, I *could* hear the sound of cars. Five o'clock traffic, buzzing along the interstate. "Is that why it's available?"

He smiled and reached for my hand as we approached the front door. "The location is actually a plus. I could be at the casinos within fifteen minutes. Assuming the road noise doesn't bother you."

I shook my head. "I can barely hear it. And the lot is beautiful."

It was. When you ignored the giant hill to one side, something I would have never noticed but that now seemed glaringly out of place, the rest was breathtaking. Lush landscaping. A valley and mountains in the background. A carved wooden ten-foot-high gate that hid us from the rest of the neighborhood. Ivy-covered walls that took over where it left off. We could have a dog here. *Two* dogs. Big ones with sharp teeth, if safety was such a concern for him.

We. My mind's slip didn't go unnoticed. *We could have a dog.* We could put goldfish in that water feature. We could decorate the house in cobwebs for Halloween and Christmas lights in December. *We* could make this a home.

The front door swung open, and a tall blonde stepped out, her smile widening at the sight of us. The agent. The last one was an uber thin gay male who used the word *fabulous* a dozen times in our tour. I hoped this one was a little less exuberant.

"Come on in." She waved us forward, and I looked past her, the interior of the home glowing with lights, the cool air conditioning floating out of the open door. "You're going to love the backyard."

I stepped into the house and felt Dario's fingers slide along the open back of my sundress, his touch possessively curling against my skin.

I stopped. "Wow."

The view was incredible. A pool that dropped off into nothing. Purple and green rolling hills, the city between us and the mountains. At night, we'd have a sea of city lights to look out on.

At night. *We.* Oh my god, I was a grown up. In a real relationship. I glanced at him and imagined waking up next to him every day. Sitting in this room and curling up next to him on the sofa. I squeezed his arm and grinned up at him.

"Wait until you see the upstairs loft. It's a bit of a cramped journey to get there, but it has a library that will blow your mind."

Dario's phone rang, and he glanced at the display, then grimaced. "Well, that's an issue. Shitty cell service in here."

I pulled out my own phone and discovered the same issue, a single bar of signal showing. As I watched, No Service flickered across the display, then the single bar returned. "Yeah, mine too."

"Once you purchase the home, you could buy a booster."

The Realtor's helpful suggestion was met with a sigh from Dario. He lifted the phone in the air and walked to the windows. "I'm going to step outside and take this."

"Let me unlock the back door for you." The realtor hurried to one of the super-tall doors, and I watched as she struggled with the lock, the cartoonish height of the door making even Dario's six-foot two-inch frame look short.

I pushed my phone back in my bag and was admiring the fireplace when the woman returned.

"Would you like to see the master suite?" She gestured toward a white stone corridor, the ceiling arched, dramatic light playing up the sides of the walls. I nodded and followed her, running my hand along the wall and admiring the old bricks.

I thought of the last place we'd seen, and all of the questions Dario had asked. "There's a security system here?"

"Oh, yes." She nodded, opening the second set of arched doors at the end of the hall. "Every window and door is alarmed, and there's a camera system that covers every inch of the three acre property."

I liked the sound of that. In my current house, my bedroom window was secured with a half-rusted nail, the screen stolen off it the summer I moved in.

"Of course, those only matter if the system is turned on." She glanced back at me with a smile but the response hit me wrong, something inside of me perking its ears up in alarm. She propped open the heavy wood door with her foot and waited for me to pass.

I stepped into the master suite and any alarm bells muted. I looked around the room and fell in love.

Dark blue walls. White stone fireplace, birch logs stacked in its hearth. White fluffy bed. Dark wooden floors. A large leather chair and ottoman, looking out on the view. I walked to the window and rested my fingertips on the glass, looking out. From this angle, I could see the pool, surrounded by manicured grounds. Just beside it, Dario, his phone to his ear, sunglasses on, looking every bit the successful man that he was. He met my eyes and I waved, a simple gesture that brought a smile to his face. He gestured to the pool area and I gave him a thumbs-up sign.

He refocused on his call, and I turned away from the window. The real estate agent had moved into the master bathroom and I followed her in, my eyes drawn to the white marble countertops, then the large shower. I eyed the bench in it and couldn't stop the image of a naked Dario, the water slick against his skin, his soapy hands on me, cleaning every inch of me.

"The bathtub overlooks the side garden. Take a look."

My cheeks colored and I moved away from the shower, turning to the tub and stopped short when I saw the woman, tucked on her side in the bottom of the huge Jacuzzi. Black dress pants and a

165

matching blazer. Dark red pumps, tucked against one side. Wrists and ankles bound in thick duct tape, two matching strips circling her face, one biting into fleshy cheeks, the other flat across her eyes.

My chest seized. I took short quick inhales that produced no oxygen whatsoever. Stumbling back, I turned, my exit blocked by the Realtor, who stepped forward with an eerily calm smile. It was the same sort of smile that Johnny had given me, that dark summer night, all of those years ago.

"You don't need to look at me like that. I could have killed her, you know."

She lifted her hand, and I saw the gun. She pulled the trigger and I jerked sideways, but it wasn't nearly fast enough.

DARIO

It was fucking hot out here. If they bought this place, they'd have to put misters in. Bring out the roofline and cover some of this deck. Blow cool air so you could enjoy the view without sweating your balls off. He adjusted his sunglasses on the bridge of his nose and settled into one of the chaise loungers, looking out on the pool. He could imagine Bell there, floating lazily by, a tiny bikini on, music playing, a drink in hand.

He glanced over his shoulder, looking at the window where he'd seen her, but the window was empty. He shifted in the seat and tried to focus on the conversation, one that had been important enough for him to step away from her.

Agent King continued. "The place was packed with people, but the wrong sort. Illegals. Hawk had them stacked like boxcars in this place. Living and working there."

"Working?" He watched as a hawk soared by, its wings tipping toward him. "What kind of work?"

"Manufacturing tourist shit. Putting together trinkets and screen printing tees. Towels. Stuff like that. There was a ton of equipment in there."

Dario grimaced, cursing himself for allowing the gift shops to remain under Hawk's wheelhouse. They had fourteen of them. Fourteen shops, all of them probably hosting now-illegal merchandise.

The agent spoke again. "ICE has the illegals. We've got a team working on that warehouse but we're moving down the list to the next prospect. The pencil pushers are still finding more locations, digging through Hawk's records. We found this parcel through his payment of the property taxes. We'll uncover a few more in that way."

Dario looked up at the late afternoon sun and thought of the heat. "You have to hurry. Who knows what kind of condition those girls are in."

He thought of Gwen, of her stories of Mexico and the dirt-floor shack where they'd kept her prisoner. The days she'd gone without water, her young body sweating valuable moisture in the humid heat. Hawk hadn't cared then, and the chances of him taking care of his prisoners now, decades later, were slim.

"I'm not gonna be able to sleep until we find them. Don't worry. We've got every spare suit on this project."

There was a sound, something from the house, and he turned his head, glancing back up at the windows. He still couldn't see her and he stood, letting his gaze drift over the back of the house, the reflection obscuring some of the rooms. "Thanks for the update. Please let me know the minute you find something."

"Will do."

Dario ended the call and headed for the back door, eager to get back to her.

TWENTY-TWO

BELL

The shot caught me in my shoulder, a thousand volts of fuck-me-up causing my body to seize, everything shaking, my collision with the floor one that I saw coming but could do absolutely nothing to stop. God, the impact hurt, the pain muted by the greater wrath of the Taser.

I had grabbed an electric fence at the barn once. It had left me disoriented, the pain more of an uncomfortable buzz, one that shattered your teeth and stole your breath. This was entirely different.

Snot ran from my nose, my heart galloped in my chest and every muscle seemed to cramp at one time. I heard a loud knocking sound and realized it was my head banging against the tile, my feet flopping into the edge of the tub, everything chattering inside my skin in the most uncomfortable manner possible.

The Realtor bitch approached, fuzzy through my tears, her blonde hair cascading down, and she had something in her hand.

I was helpless, unable to fight, unable to think, unable to do anything but watch through blurry eyes as a sharp pain jabbed into my bare thigh.

She stabbed me. The thought came and then, pleasantly enough, I had no thoughts at all.

DARIO

The back door, the one the Realtor had let him out through, was locked. He pulled at the handle, one that had a keypad on the dial, and cursed the security system that had brought him here to begin with. She should have taken him through one of the sliding doors, those giant masterpieces that had set someone back a fortune. He could have left it open and be jogging up the stairs to the second floor right now. But between the FBI's number showing up on the screen, and the heat from outside, he'd stepped out and pulled the door firmly to, wanting privacy for the call. Now, he was stuck out here like an idiot.

He cupped his hands and peered in, banging on the glass with his fist. Shielding the glare with his palm, he looked over the great room and kitchen. No sign of them. They were probably still down that stone hall, still in the master suite. He stepped back, to his place by the pool and squinted up at the windows to the master suite, hoping to see one of them cross. Nothing. Unease began to set in. Unlocking his phone, he called Bell's, growling in frustration when the voicemail picked right up. Thumbing through his contacts, he tried the agent. Same result. *Fuck*.

They'd have to come out of there eventually. Pass through the living room. Look at the kitchen before crossing to the other side of the house. He returned to the door and leaned against the glass, taking another visual tour of the space. Any minute.

A minute passed. Then two. He pounded on the glass again. Yelled out loud like a lunatic. Finally, he gave up on the back doors and stepped off the back deck, trudging across the manicured grass and through a planter, moving purposely toward the side of the house. *Screw it.* He'd go around front.

He was stopped by the wall. Ten feet high and covered in ivy, designed to keep intruders out. Another security selling point, one the sales brochure had gushed over and he now vehemently hated. He was rolling up his sleeves, examining the brick obstacle with the practiced eye of an athlete, when he heard the engine.

He stilled, holding his breath and listened, trying to decipher the sounds. It wasn't a lawnmower. Too powerful for that. There was the pop of a clutch and his irritation bloomed into worry. He knew that sound. Every boy in Louisiana knew the sound of a four-wheeler popped into gear. There was the clatter of a garage door opening, the roll of hinges and metal, and his worry manifested into fear.

There was no good reason for a four-wheeler to be started right now, not unless Mrs. Fucking Realtor planned on a desert tour, and she wouldn't have done that without getting him. *Something was wrong.* He backed up and screamed Bell's name. Ran forward, his dress shoes slipping on the damp grass and hurtled himself at the wall. He grappled with vines and slick soles and made it halfway up before falling. The engine revved, moving, and he screamed her name again, scrambling to his feet and back at the wall, his nails digging into stone, his muscles bunching, pulling, working him up the solid face. He got one hand to the top, finding the iron spikes that helped, giving him a handle. His forearms flexed and he hoisted himself to his waist, getting his first clear view of the front yard.

An open garage door.

The realtor's minivan, still parked at an angle.

The Lambo, still in place.

The drone of the four-wheeler grew faint.

He pulled himself over, the spikes of the wall catching on and ripping his shirt. He fell down the face of the ivy, hitting the ground, his knee screaming in protest.

Everything was still. Everything looked normal.

Except, of course, everything wasn't.

🂠

THE REALTOR

One of her first lessons was from Tanaka Kangara. They'd grown up together. Like sisters, only Tanaka was black, and she was white, and they were only two months apart in age. Both with moms who didn't care enough, both with dads they didn't know. Both liked Jerry Springer after school, hidden under the bench in Lorna Pulley's sewing shop. Ms. Lorna worked her embroidery machine and ignored them, her ridiculously long legs stretched out, inches from their faces as she pressed down on the pedal, the needles whirring to action above them.

In middle school, they'd been allies, their arms linked in stubborn support as they'd negotiated through the crowded hallways of Vegas's worst school system. In high school, they'd all but abandoned their mothers, staying out late, dating older men, and scheming over their futures, ones out of the projects and closer to the glam of the Vegas Strip.

Tanaka had tutored her through her struggles with algebra. She'd taught her how to create the perfect smoky eye. She'd taught her how to flirt, how to lie smoother than butter and how to distract a mark from deception. And Tanaka had taught her, when she was begging for her life, how *not* to die.

And Robert Hawk, in killing Tanaka, had shown her how to truly rip someone's heart out. You could only hurt someone so much with pain. You could kill them slowly, *kill* every bit of humanity and happiness in their soul, when you took away the ones they love. When you *killed* the ones they loved. It was a lesson she had never forgotten, and one she would use on Bell and Dario.

The four-wheeler climbed up the berm easily, moving in between the thick trees, branching occasionally slapping against her chest. Before them, the sounds of the highway increased. She heard a shout, and didn't look back, increasing her speed, the excitement burning through her chest.

Mounting the berm, the ATV wove through the tree line and reached the highway. She released the throttle and it rolled to a stop next to her SUV. Reaching into her pocket, she pressed the button on the fob and popped open the rear hatch. She crouched beside the back rack and carefully maneuvered Bell Hartley's limp body over her shoulder. Using her legs, she straightened, carrying her, fireman-style, to the back of the SUV and unloading her into the back of it. Closing the trunk, she abandoned the ATV and stepped into the vehicle.

Thirty seconds later, they were on the road and heading to the warehouse.

DARIO

She was his world. If something happened, if she was harmed ... his chest constricted at the possibilities. He jabbed at the screen of his phone, calling 9-1-1 and staring up at the berm, the tracks from the ATV fresh on the grass. Fuck these rich prick rentals with their house full of toys. And fuck him for driving the Lambo. That car would go ten feet across grass and get stuck. He listened to the phone ring and jerked at the minivan handle, the car locked, a useless option anyway.

The emergency operator answered, and he barked out the situation.

His mind warred between storming up the berm, chasing the ATV tracks, and breaking down the front door to see if Bell was inside. She might be there, hurt, scared, needing him.

The other possibility made his eyes close, his face muscles tensing as he fought for control. *She could be in there, dead.* Whoever this bitch was, whatever had just happened, he had to fix this. He had to fix *everything* and he couldn't even fucking decide which path to take. The berm or the house. He looked back and forth and spat out directions to the operator, ordering a roadblock on the highway, something that would probably happen ten minutes too late. If she had a vehicle there, hidden in the trees, just off the interstate... she could be inside it by now. She could be driving away and laughing, with Bell's blood on her hands.

The image had him striding to the front door, the handle locked, his foot lifting and stomping at the jam. It took three kicks and the wood splintered. Another two and he was inside, his breath coming in spurts, his fear almost crushing in its intensity.

Dread hit when he heard the silence in the home. No screams of pain, no calls for help. If she was here... If she *wasn't* here, he was wasting time and risking her life. He forced his feet to move, his voice to work, his call of her name wobbly and weak. He pushed through the arched doorway and ran down the hall and into the master bedroom.

He stopped short, the room pristine, his gaze scanning over everything in an instance. He moved to the bathroom, pushing open the door, almost paralyzed with the thought of what might lay behind it.

She was his everything. His heart. His soul. His future. His life.

He stepped inside and saw her sandal, lying on its side, alone on a stretch of empty white tile. *No. No. No. Not again.*

TWENTY-THREE

BELL

My head was dying. I had a million needles jabbing into my temples, and my eyes wouldn't open. I was trying, working every tiny muscle behind those lids, and nothing happened. I attempted to roll over, to bring my tongue back inside my mouth, but I couldn't do that either.

I'm paralyzed. The thought was blindingly apparent, and panic flared. Only, I couldn't move. I couldn't scream, I couldn't do anything to react, and that was even more maddening.

But I *could* feel. I could feel how dry my throat was, my tongue heavy. I could feel a glob of saliva, saliva I desperately needed, running along my open lips and dripping to the floor. I could feel the painful bite of the metal cuffs, cuffs that were stretching my arms out, my shoulders aching from the strain. I checked in with my lower half and found my legs splayed out, my butt on the floor.

I don't think paralyzed people can feel pain. It's both a blessing and a curse. Maybe I wasn't paralyzed. But, then again, paralysis would cause me to be immune to whatever hell was before me. Instead, I might feel it all. And I had an inkling this blonde bitch had all sorts of crazy shit planned for me.

Speaking of which ... I focused on the sounds in the room. Someone was in here with me. I could hear footsteps. Confident ones. Moving right to left. Something crackled, plastic wrapping removed off an unknown item. *Dario*. Was he here also? Had she had more people in the house, waiting? Did they take him?

An item was moved, the long squeak of friction sounding against the floor. I struggled to open my eyes. One of them moved a smidgen, enough to give me a hazy look at white concrete. I couldn't see her, but my senses seemed to be returning. I strained again to open my eyes and was rewarded with a wedge of light, a cloudy figure nearby. The Realtor. She was bent over something, her long blonde hair draped close to the floor.

She came closer and stopped before me. I tried to lift my head but it didn't move. From this angle, I could see one ripped knee on a pair of faded jeans. I thought back, of her welcoming us into the house, the conservative skirt and blazer. She'd changed. I wondered when she did that. I wondered how long I'd been drooling all over the place and hanging here like a broken marionette puppet.

Her foot lifted and I saw the black combat boot it wore. My eye opened a little bit more and I managed a blink. She pushed her boot into my chest and the treads of the shoe bit painfully into my breasts. I wheezed out a pained cry.

Ah. So, I could talk. My tongue twitched, and I managed to pull it into my mouth, swallowing a painful gulp that did nothing to ease my thirst. Why was I so thirsty? How long had it been? An hour? A day? I had no concept of time.

"Water." My voice didn't sound like me. It sounded old and feeble.

My tongue felt sandpapery and this must be how a cat feels, all of the time.

She laughed and I tried to figure out what she was laughing about. Had I said something? I couldn't remember.

She pulled back her boot from my chest and my eyelids finally worked, dragging apart.

DARIO

Uniforms swarmed the mini-mansion, LVPD in white letters that seemed to scream at him from every vest. Dario stood in the grand living room and made the call, his fifth in the last hour. Finally, this time, the man picked up.

"I can't keep holding your hand with updates. We're working on this. You have to be patient. This guy—"

"She took Bell. Kidnapped her."

There was a beat of silence, then the federal agent spoke. "Bell Hartley? *Who* took her?"

"A blonde. Tall. We had an appointment to look at a house. She tied up the realtor and posed as her. I stepped out of the house to talk to you, and that's when she took her."

"Is there blood?"

Dario knew what the man was really asking. After all, Gwen's killer hadn't been concerned with kidnapping. Death had been the focus there. So why, this time, was it different? The woman would have had plenty of time to shoot Bell and take off. But she didn't. She took Bell *with* her. Why?

He shook his head. "There wasn't any blood. A shoe—Bell's sandal —was left behind. And her purse was tossed in the tub with the Realtor. Nothing else. There's a highway that runs adjacent to this house. It looks like she took her there and had a car waiting."

"This doesn't make sense. Do you think she was hired? That she's the one who hit Gwen?" Agent King asked.

Dario pinched the bridge of his nose, trying to remember some-thing, *anything*, about the woman who had let them into the house. But any woman had paled next to Bell, and his eyes had swept over her without looking, her greeting barely acknowledged, her chatter about the house, the bedrooms, the lot—all ignored.

She had been blonde. Fairly tall. A thin muscular build. That was all he could remember about her. A sketch artist would be arriving any minute to work with him on a drawing, and he was coming up blank with regards to her face. Had he shook her hand? Looked her in the eye? Introduced himself?

"Dario? You there?"

He tried to refocus on the conversation. *Do you think she was hired? That she's the one who hit Gwen?* He shook his head. "I don't know. Who the fuck would want to hurt her now that Hawk was dead? I don't know—" He shook his head. "I don't know what is happening."

It didn't make sense. Hawk's goons were all hired muscle. There was no devotion among his crew, no personal interests in his successes, other than the promise of a paycheck. With his death, the money stopped. Any jobs in progress would have died with the vanishing of their reward.

The knowledge of that had caused Dario to become lax. He'd thought that when he was with her, she was protected. He'd lined up bodyguards to cover her the rest of the time. Instead, he should have gone into full security mode. A team following them. A trackable device on her person. Their destinations secured in advance. A level of protection that rivaled the Secret Service.

The agent's voice dropped into an apologetic tone. "We're tied up with this warehouse search. I don't have assets to reassign to look for your girlfriend."

Dario fought the urge to reach out and punch the nearest wall. "These are connected. For all we know, she's taking Bell to the warehouse now. This is your hottest lead, and it's fresh."

So fresh he could still smell Bell's perfume. So fresh that the sound of the ATV seemed to hum in his ear. Why had he taken the call? Why had he shut the door? Why had he left her alone and thought she'd be safe?

Because it was a woman. A sexist move that had cost him everything. He saw a woman and dismissed her as a threat. He dismissed her, and the moment his back had turned, she had struck.

"Chances are, she's not taking Bell to the warehouse. Chances are that she's taking her somewhere remote. Come on, Dario. You know this."

The softening of his voice did nothing to cushion the vision he created. Somewhere remote where she would be hurt. Somewhere she'd scream, and no one would hear. Someone that she'd be scared and he wouldn't be there to save, comfort, and protect her.

The thought was a knife to Dario's gut.

BELL

I was close to vomiting. I willed my stomach to calm, the pitch and coil of it to lessen, and watched the darkness, catching the moment the shadows shifted and the woman re-entered the cell. Still no sign of Dario, no mention of him. I wanted to know, but I was afraid to ask.

"Who are you?" I rasped out the question, my throat still dry, my repeated requests for water ignored. I had wanted a friendly tone, but it came out wrong. Hard. Accusatory. Then again, any chance of a friendship between us had dried up around the time she Tased me.

She ignored my question, moving to the far end of the cell, and I noticed the other door. Through the open entrance and across the hall. *Another cell*. Like this one. I struggled to bring my feet underneath me, fighting against the cuffs until I managed to get my soles flat, my body rising... I got a glimpse of another dark head, *a girl*, and then my ankles caved, my legs too rubbery. I fell forward, the cuffs yanking me back right before my head hit the concrete floor.

"Careful." The woman carried a metal folding chair, and set it up in front of me.

"Who's that?" I lifted my chin and tried my best to use it to point to the opposite cell, my sluggish mind putting together some of the pieces. Remembering what Dario had told me. This had been the first stop on Robert Hawk's prisoner's journey. A warehouse with captured women. But Hawk was dead.

"Ignore her." She sat in the chair and flipped on a penlight, bringing it up to my face. The light was blinding, and I winced, closing my eyes to it.

"It hurts, doesn't it? The light?" She brought it closer to me. "I was right here once. Just like you. Only, unlike you, I didn't deserve it."

I wet my lips. Tried to swallow. Listened to her and hoped that a lecture was all that she had planned.

"We were so close," she whispered. "All you had to do was die, and everything was going to be okay."

Her words were so soft that I almost missed them, the light coming too close to my pupil. I pinched my eyes shut in defense.

"Do you know what you did wrong, Bell?"

Yeah, I knew what I did wrong. *Trusted this crazy bitch to show me a bathroom without incapacitating me.* That was the first thing that came to mind. But other than that, there was only one thing I could think of, at least in terms of landing me in Robert Hawk's warehouse. *Dario.*

I wet my lips. "Dario."

She turned off the light and I blinked rapidly, trying to see past the dots in my vision, trying to get a good look at her face.

"You disrespected my family."

She bent over and reached in the canvas bag that sat by the foot of the chair.

"You made me look like a failure in front of my father."

When she straightened, she held an item that made my nausea swell.

"He died before seeing my mistake righted."

She rose to her feet and flipped the knife over in her hand,

"Which means, pretty little, sweet little, slutty little Bell..." She leaned forward until her hair brushed my neck, her mouth close to my ear. "You're going to have to pay for all that. Pay for it, and punish Dario... All. At. Once."

TWENTY-FOUR

DARIO

Three hours passed. Three hours where roadblocks were set up, traffic footage reviewed, fingerprint teams dusted powder over everything, and a bunch of LVPD officers stood around with their dicks in their hands. They had nothing. No fingerprints except for his and Bell's. A face sketch that wasn't worth the paper it was drawn on. No vehicle description or other leads. The Realtor—the *real* Realtor—was useless. She'd been walking through the house, turning on lights, the front door unlocked, when someone had come up behind her. Slapped duct tape over her eyes and mouth, easily controlled her attempts to fight, and carried her into the bathroom and dropped her in the tub, injecting her with a sedative of some form. The woman was strong. They knew that. The rest was one giant fucking question mark.

Dario tore the car through the streets, then parked diagonally across two spots outside the police station. Let them fucking ticket or tow it. He plowed through the door, ignored the desk attendant, and moved down the side hall, beelining to the room that housed the FBI task force.

Fucking feds. He'd hated them when they'd stormed The Majestic six years ago and tried to pin shit on them, and he hated them now. Hated that frazzled look that Agent King shot him, as if he didn't have time for Dario, or want his help. Fuck *all* of that.

He stopped beside the board, a giant map of Las Vegas and the surrounding hundred miles, and stared at the circled areas. "Tell me what you've got."

Agent King sighed, turning around and grabbing at a folder, flipping it open and pointing to the first red circle on the map. "This is our best possibility. He purchased the raw land six years ago and built a twenty-thousand square foot structure on it. Place is pulling a fair amount of electricity per month, so something is happening there, we just aren't sure of what. Drones are headed that way to see what kind of heat signatures are coming from inside."

"This is your best possibility. How many do you have?" Dario asked.

"Four that look promising."

The agent worked through each one of them. Number two was an old car parts factory, eight miles outside of Vegas, on the edge of an abandoned exit. Number three was a horse farm with a ten-thousand square feet barn and underground bunker. And the last one was thirty-seven miles outside of Vegas, a property listed as a water filtration plant and squatted in the middle of a two-hundred-acre lot.

Dario took a deep breath, struggling to cool his head and find some bit of control. *He needed to get to Bell.* But all he could see was red. Pure fury, something he had to harness amidst Hawk's barbarity. He focused on the list, forcing himself to close out the pain and use the anger productively.

Dario looked over the options. "The horse farm isn't it. Gwen and I went by there a few years ago. She wanted to have a ranch closer to home. It's a glorified shooting range. Which isn't to say that Hawk hasn't done some fucked up things out there, but the barn was practically a tear-down, covered in cobwebs and dust. He wasn't using it then, that's for sure."

He pulled the folder from the man's hand and flipped through the pages. "And the car factory isn't right." He pointed to the property map of the factory, his finger tapping on the adjacent parcel. "That's a military base. He wouldn't be that close to someone who pays attention."

He focused on the map, his hands flipping through to the aerial shots of the two remaining prospects. Both isolated parcels, no neighbors close by. Both buildings large, set in the middle of the land, with no trees or cover to hide behind. It would be a bitch to sneak up on either, which would be perfect for Hawk's needs.

The FBI agent circled the perimeter of each lot with the tip of his index finger. "They're both fenced in lots. High, military-grade fencing. The sort that would cause the average lost or nosy visitor to wander away." He nodded to the discarded options. "For the record, your opinion on those two just helps to confirm our own thoughts. The likelihood is, one of these two locations is where they're at. The pencil pushers are running dry on any other options, and they've looked at just about every industrial structure in the state."

He met Dario's eyes. "You know, these warehouses could be unrelated to Bell Hartley's disappearance. We could find the girls, and not her."

"I know that." Dario stared at the map. The pieces *had* to be connected. They'd find the warehouse, reunite him with Bell, arrest that woman ... and they'd get the answers. For now, he needed to focus on one task at a time and forget any other, less optimistic, possibility.

He *would* find her. He *would* save her.

There was no other option.

BELL

"Don't worry. I'm not going to cut you just yet." The girl sat down on the folding chair.

Just yet. Talk about a barely reassuring statement. I watched her reach back into the bag and tensed, wondering what she'd pull out next. The Taser? A gun? Maybe another needle. Truth be told, the idea of being pricked and sleeping for the next few hours wasn't a bad option. I thought of Dario's treatment of John and Johnny, his castration of them, and felt the urge to vomit.

Maybe we deserved this. Ruining his marriage. Exacting revenge. Maybe everything had led to this moment.

The blonde pulled out a pad of paper and a pen.

My heartbeat slowed slightly, and I allowed myself a full inhalation of air.

She flipped the knife over, sticking it butt-first into her back pocket. Moving closer, she tugged at a key that hung around her neck, pulling it over her head. She looked down at me. "Are you left or right-handed?"

A simple question, yet my mind stalled. *Left or right-handed?* Seconds passed. Her expression hardened and I forced myself to speak.

"Right-handed."

She dropped the paper and pen on the floor next to me and crouched down until her butt rested on her heels. Working the key into the cuff on my right hand, she popped the mechanism, the restraint springing open. I cautiously rolled the wrist, flexing my hand as she stepped away and brought the knife back out.

She nodded to the items beside me. "Pick up the pen and paper. I want you to write a letter."

I didn't move toward the paper. "A letter to who?"

She smiled, and it was the sort of grin that fit better on a Halloween mask than a face.

THE BOSS

As Bell wrote, Claudia began to pace. It was a useless activity, a waste of energy, and she stopped short, forcing herself to step back, her hands clasped before her, her restlessness under control. If Robert was here, he'd have given her a nod of approval, the sort that caused her heart to swell and her efforts to double. He wasn't cruel. She had seen it early, had understood the difference between punishment and sadism. He'd always had a purpose behind his actions, a plan in place, a lesson to be learned. A lesson that went right over the heads of almost every woman in this place. He should have just killed them all, but that wasn't his style. Instead, he had an almost dogged determination to break through to them. To give them opportunities, again and again, over and over again. Punishments and lessons. Reward opportunities and tests.

Most had failed completely. Others, like the ones in this building, had succeeded often enough to stay alive. Claudia was the *only* one who had truly understood Hawk's methods, and it certainly made sense why. She was special, and not just because of her lineage. Gwen had Robert Hawk's blood in her, and she would have failed. Claudia knew that, the instinct reinforced by the stories Robert had told her. Stories of a baby Gwen, bullied at school. Gwen, in Mexico, needing rescue. Gwen, marrying a man and letting him take control of her life.

The brunette was being slow, the slanted writing only covering half of the page.

She sighed. "You've got two more minutes, then you're done. So write it quickly or don't say it at all."

Bell's pen scratched more quickly across the surface. It was cute, all of the thought she was putting into this. Cute, the dogged concentration on her face, the intent desire to flood all of her feelings onto the page. Robert Hawk hadn't had that luxury, hadn't had the chance to say goodbye to anyone. Which was one reason out of a hundred that solidified her decision to use this letter like a knife. She'd present it to Dario, wave the emotional tidbit in front of him, and then snatch it away before he had a chance to read it. Light his love's final words on fire and watch him drop to his knees in tears. Then, she'd bring out the video, and let him watch every excruciating minute of Bell Hartley's final day.

It'd be a good day. A long day. One of those Robert Hawk specials. Maybe she'd bring in a prop. Borrow one of the other prisoners and let Bell Hartley watch everything that she was about to do to her. After all, she'd been trained by the best—a walking encyclopedia of torture.

What she hadn't decided yet, was whether to finish the girl's kill on videotape, or wait for that final finale until she had Dario here. Decisions, decisions. Decisions that she should have made hours ago, but was still waffling over.

She leaned over and snatched the page from Bell's hand, the last word not fully formed. No biggie. He wouldn't be reading it anyway.

She left the right handcuff off and sat down on the folding chair, lifting the page and reading the cramped cursive writing.

Dario,

I'm not scared. I want you to know that, if anything happens to me, that I'm not scared. And I don't regret anything. If I had to do everything all over again, I'd still walk up those steps to see you in that club. I'd still let you kiss me. I'd return your texts. I'd come to that suite in the middle of the night. I don't regret anything except that I wish I'd had more time with you. I wish I'd moved in to that suite, the moment you gave me the code. I wish I hadn't gone to Louisiana, but stayed beside you throughout all that you had to endure. I wish I'd had a hundred more nights with you, a hundred more days, a hundred more kisses.

I know my death will bring you pain, but don't let it bring you guilt. Or regret. Or any more pain than it needs to. I knew what I was getting into. I would make the same choices now, because I will never regret getting the chance to love you. To be loved by you. It's been the greatest blessing of my life. I love you.

Forever yours,

Be—

Forever yours. Cute. Her hand tightened on the knife and she pushed herself to her feet, the letter fluttering to the ground. This girl thought that she loved him, but she didn't. She told him that she wasn't scared, but she was. She thought that she'd made the right decision, destroying the marriage of a *Hawk?*

Wrong statement to make, stupid girl.

Forever yours was going to be a very, very short time.

TWENTY-FIVE

DARIO

Dario hung up the phone, letting out a frustrated breath. The heat signatures on the first warehouse had come back. Live bodies inside, and that was enough to cause a full monopoly of their attention. The agents were now coordinating with local SWAT, a process that had gotten him escorted to the door, thanks to his civilian status. He leaned against the back wall of the police station and scrolled through his phone, working through a new plan.

"Hey."

Dario looked up, recognizing the blond friend of Bell's. *Lance.* Beside him stood the other one. "Hey. No word yet."

He wasn't surprised to see them, his eyes moving past them and to the large Humvee taking up a spot and a half. Some mental gears clicked into place.

"Anything we can do to help?" Rick asked.

A gate to the left opened, a SWAT van slowly rolling out, followed by a second vehicle. The men watched the action, looking to Dario for clarity.

Dario nodded slowly. "They're headed to a potential location, one that might hold some of Hawk's pets."

"And Bell?" Lance asked.

In the tone of those two words, Dario heard all that he had suspected. This man, probably both of them, loved her like a sister. They were as afraid as he was. As invested and frustrated as he was.

Dario tucked his hands into his pockets. "Maybe. We don't know. I'm hoping that the woman who took her is connected to the warehouse in some way. Otherwise—"

Otherwise, they didn't have shit to go on.

Otherwise, the chance of saving Bell was nil.

Rick flipped his keys over in his hands. "You know where they're going?"

His eyes met Dario's, and Dario nodded.

"Then, let's fucking go," Lance said.

"Wait." Dario reached out and grabbed Lance's arm. "They're going to their best prospect. But there is another option, a different place she might be. They didn't have the manpower to hit both locations, so they're going to the most likely first."

It was a risk to get involved with them, bringing them into a scenario that he was still figuring out for himself. But the men didn't hesitate.

"We've got guns. Vests. Rocket launchers. Pretty much anything they have in there." Rick offered. "If you know where the second location is, let's head there. Cover all possibilities as quickly as possible."

Dario gave them a final lifeline. "The Feds aren't going to like that, us using their intel to break into private property, weapons drawn."

Lance scrunched up his face, looking up at the sky as if to consider the ramifications. Then he dropped his gaze back to Dario's and shrugged. "Checked, and nope. No fucks given."

He glanced over at his friend. "Rick? You? Any fucks given?"

The man grinned and slapped his hand on Lance's shoulder. "Nope. Let's do this shit."

Dario, for the first time in four hours, felt his own mouth curve into a smile.

"Good. I'll make a few calls. I have some resources we can call in." *Hang on, Bell. Please, for the love of God, be strong and hang on.*

It was night in Vegas. A clusterfuck of photo-taking tourists and restaurant-seeking locals. For the first time in a decade, Dario cursed his premiere real estate locations, set in the heart of The Strip. He was in his own version of Lance's Hummer, a Land Rover Defender that hadn't been off the showroom floor but could crawl over a wall if need be. He pulled out of The Majestic's parking garage followed by six company SUVs, each one packed with the best private security that Vegas offered. There was a reason retired Special Forces gravitated to Vegas. Pussy and pay. He had always paid the most, and they could trip over pussy leaving work each day. Now, with fourteen ex-military bad-asses behind him, they rivaled anything the LVPD was sending to the other location.

She had to be in one of these two locations, safe and waiting for him. He couldn't handle any other possibility.

"You're leaving The Majestic unprotected." His head of security shifted in the seat, pulling the phone away from his mouth to deliver the opinion. "Someone comes in, wants to clean us out? Now would be the time to do it."

Dario shrugged. The Majestic was the last thing on his list of concerns. He got onto the highway, his throat tightening at the knowledge that they'd pass the location, just a few miles ahead, where Bell had been put into a car and taken away.

Was she in pain right now? Was she scared? Each minute that passed felt interminable. Who was this woman? And why the fuck, of all things to do, would she take Bell?

Tire track analysis had put the bitch's vehicle as a large SUV. A Yukon, Suburban, Escalade or Expedition. It was a classification that barely narrowed things down, especially in this town. His phone buzzed and he reached for it, opening the incoming text message. It was from Laurent.

—Landed. Where do you need me?

Dario swallowed the emotion that unexpectedly thickened in his throat. Sometimes, the people you *didn't* call were the ones you needed the most.

BELL

This bitch was crazy. I hadn't taken her opinions into consideration when I'd written the letter to Dario. I'd been thinking only of his mindset, and how he would feel and react if I died. I was trying to calm his fears and lessen any guilt. I wasn't thinking about her reading it, and certainly hadn't expected the reaction it created.

She shoved to her feet, holding the page out, the wide-lined page trembling from her outstretched fingers. Night had fallen and taken most of the light with it. I peered at her through the dimness and tried to understand the rigid set of her body. I think she was angry. I thought back over my letter, trying to see what I might have written that would have caused that emotion.

Then, I thought over what she had said to me.

"We were so close," she had whispered. "All you had to do was die, and everything was going to be okay."

The *we* of the statement had stuck with me, almost as much as her mention of her father, his disappointment, his death... it had all pointed in one giant arrow to Robert Hawk. The devil. Who, possibly... passed his evil down to this woman.

Or, she was delusional. Or, just as likely, both.

"It's cute that you think you love him. But Gwen... Gwen loved him too." Her dark outline stepped closer. I couldn't see the expression on her face, but her voice was a mix of amusement and disgust. In her question, Gwen's name stood out as if it was printed in Las Vegas neon. Her one-syllable name had been said with reverence, the sentence arching up to that finish, as if no one should dare to offend GWEN.

This was personal. Whatever dynamic I'd entered into when I'd first kissed, touched, and fell for Dario ... the girl had been part of that dynamic. Maybe we were wrong. Maybe Hawk hadn't ordered the hit. Maybe this girl had had her own agenda, her own role that had played out in this disaster.

"We were so close..."

She reached forward and I saw the glint of the knife in the moment before she scraped the blade's tip along my outer thigh. "Listen, you spoiled slutty Vegas whore. You don't *get* to love Dario Capece. And he doesn't get to fuck around without having serious consequences brought down on his shoulders."

I could see the white flash of her teeth when she smiled.

"Robert," she drawled. "Before he died, before you all TOOK HIM FROM ME..."

The blade bit into my thigh, her weight toying with the pressure, and I gasped at the pain, my mind scrambling for time, for a way to distract her with conversation. "I know you killed her."

It was a wild card, and probably untrue, but it worked. The knife stilled, the pain dulling, and the dark shadow tilted her head. "You don't know what I've done. What I've been through. What I've SACRIFICED." She moved closer, her breath hot on my face.

I had bought a few seconds, nothing more. I kept my right hand still, hidden by my side, and hoped she had forgotten about it. I needed to do something. Right now. Something to stop her.

I thought of the martial arts lessons I took freshman semester. Tried to find something that my free hand might be useful for. *Box her on the ears.* That might give me about five seconds of time. Cup my hand, swing it around, putting the force of my body into the motion ... she'd fall to the side and experience a few seconds of disorientation.

But a few seconds was useless when I was chained to the wall by my other hand. I tried to remember what she had done with the handcuff key. Had she returned it to her neck? Was it over in the bag? Was it still hanging from the handcuffs? I couldn't risk looking, broadcasting my search, especially not right now, with her staring at me, *waiting* for me to respond to her psychotic dialog.

I couldn't *think*, couldn't come up with something to say. She was right. I didn't know what she'd done. Or been through. Or sacrificed. I'd say this. I was raped by two men when I was fourteen and had managed to maintain a normal life. She was in a warehouse full of prisoners, shoving a knife into my thigh. I was going to guess she had been through hell and back to fall to this point.

She prodded, unhappy with my lack of response. "You think you

KNOW ME?"

She pushed on the knife, and it effortlessly cut deeper into the muscle, severing nerves and lighting my thigh on fire. I screamed, the pain blotting out my vision, the intensity worse, so much worse, than the initial penetration had been.

"Please." I wheezed out the word, my chained hand gripping my thigh just above the place where the knife jutted out of it. Blood bubbled around the blade, running down my muscle. Too much blood. Didn't I have a major artery somewhere in my thigh? The femoral? What if she hit it? I could be minutes from bleeding out. *Minutes from death.*

"You think I killed Gwen? *Please.*" She stood. "YOU killed Gwen." She lifted one boot and hovered it gently in the air about the knife. "Think I can get it to go all the way through? One hard stomp, I think it'll do it. Can we at least try? I've always wanted to try."

She giggled, then stopped, her silhouette suddenly illuminated in bright red light. Her head twisted around, the long blonde strands spinning out, and eyed the overhead bulb that had illuminated. I watched her boot carefully, my heart in my throat as the heavy black rubber sole swayed above the wooden handle. The light began to blink, dousing the room in black, then red, then black, then red.

Her head snapped toward the light and she paused for a moment, watching it flash. "Shit."

There was a crash, a deep engine revving, and the terrible grind of metal against metal. I looked in the direction of the sound, trying to gauge how far away it was, hoping that it was somehow tied to the red light.

When I looked back, she was gone and I was alone in the room, the knife still protruding from my bloody thigh. I locked my free hand around my thigh and tried to staunch the bleeding.

TWENTY-SIX

THE REACTOR

Shit. Claudia ran up the stairs and to the small room at the top landing, entering the code and shoving open the door. She leaned over the desk, her eyes darting over the grid of camera screens until she found the right one. A Humvee had broken through the fence on the east end. The night vision camera showed bodies moving, crawling over the vehicle and stepping over the electric wire. She spun, looking at the cameras facing the opposite end of the property, and saw another set of SUVs pull up there. *Motherfuckers.*

She watched the men as they crossed into another camera's line of vision, their guns drawn, night vision goggles on. The view went black, then static, the connection gone, the camera taken out. As she watched, another monitor flashed dark, then white. *She was running out of time.* She straightened, looking around the room, thinking through the evidence that may exist. There were no files, no names, nothing in the room that connected her to him. Her eyes fell on a scrap of magazine, one she'd taped to the desk. She reached forward and carefully pulled it off the surface. It was a photo of Robert, taken years ago, around the time he'd brought her in. It had been published in a Vegas social publication, the image taken at a benefit, and it was one of the few photos she'd ever seen of him. He was smiling in the photo. Genuinely smiling. It was a beautiful and rare thing for her to see, especially on him and she looked at it whenever she needed a reminder of the man that lurked behind the hard exterior.

In the last four years, he had become the focus of her entire world. A focus honed and sharpened in their joint pursuit of... She inhaled sharply, her mind unraveling, his lessons already flaking, dissolving, her mind twisting into knots ever since. She hadn't killed Gwen. She couldn't have killed Gwen. Everything that she had said to Bell Hartley was true.

She killed Gwen. They killed Gwen. They both, in evil concert with Nick Fentes, killed Gwen and then Robert. Her family. Her family, which she had been just days, just moments, away from fully joining.

The interior alarm blared, a motion sensor tripped, and they, this brigade of men and guns and disaster—were here.

She had only minutes to make a decision. Run? Fight? Or...

Her focus settled in. *Deceive.*

She eyed the broken cameras, imagining the soldiers circling the building, advancing closer. Guns drawn. Twenty or thirty of them against her. Escape would be all but impossible. Except that, she knew exactly how to do it.

Reaching up, she gripped the top of her head and yanked. The blonde wig peeled away and fell to the floor.

BELL

The red light stopped, the cell falling back into darkness. I held my breath and listened, straining my ears in the direction that the crash had come from. What had it been? It hadn't come from inside the warehouse. It had sounded further away. Almost *too* far away. Maybe it was a car accident on the closest road.

I heard the clatter of shoes, pounding down a stairwell, inside the structure. I tensed, my eyes on the front of the cell, and waited for her to reappear.

Nothing happened. The footsteps ceased, her path taking her somewhere else. Silence grew, and I wondered why this place was so quiet. Didn't the other women *say* anything? Did they all just sit there in silence, all day long?

My thigh throbbed with pain, drawing my attention back to the knife still sticking out from my thigh. I took a long, shuddering breath and gently touched the area around the wound. My fingers came away damp and warm and I felt lightheaded, unsure if it was due to blood loss or anxiety. I could feel the blood dripping down my thigh, a pool of it forming under my leg. How much blood could I lose? I took quick short breaths and regripped my upper thigh, second-guessing the motion when more blood seemed to pool around the blade.

Something banged once, twice, and then a loud third time. I stilled, my head raised, and listened. A battering ram? The quiet returned and I yanked at my cuffed hand, testing the restraint, my gaze frantically searching over the ground, the other cuff, looking for the handcuff key. She was going to come back. She was going to come back and she'd kill me. Kill me in the final second before they found us. I froze when, through the dark open door of the cell, a flashlight beam cut through the darkness. I straightened and watched as its beam floated over a concrete pillar. My chest constricted. I hesitated, warring between silence and screaming. I took in a deep breath. "Hello?"

In my head, my call of greeting had been a shout. But it came out weak, my voice wobbling on the final note, the end result something barely audible, and not nearly loud enough. The cell walls swallowed the call, and I repeated the word, this time louder, as loud as I could manage. The flashlight clicked off. A door creaked open. I held my breath as a dark body eased in front of my cell, one step carefully placed in front of the other, a gun held out, sweeping across my cell. *A cop*. I sank against the concrete wall, relief seizing my chest. The man held a finger in front of his mouth and I nodded. He stepped forward, continuing on. The next figure, even in the dark, even with goggles on and features obscured, I knew. I knew it in the broad width of his shoulders. The strength of his frame. The height. The confidence in his movements. He came into the cell with quick steps and crouched beside me, pulling me into his arms.

Dario.

He brought me into his chest and the scent of him, the strong squeeze of him .... I clutched at him with my free hand, a shuddering exhale bubbling out of me. He pulled off his night-vision goggles and kissed me everywhere. Strong presses of his lips on the top of my head, my forehead, cheeks, lips. He whispered my name and I cupped his face, my nails digging into the short stubble of his beard, then his shoulders, then across his chest.

He saw the knife and froze. "Oh my God. Bell."

I gripped his shirt, pulling his eyes to mine. "It's okay. It looks worse than it is."

"It looks like a shitload of blood. We need to get you to a doctor. I've got someone here, let me get him—" He started to stand and I yanked at his shirt, keeping him down.

"Don't leave me. *Please*. Just wait."

He kissed me again, his hand tightening on the back of my head. "I'll stay. I love you. God, I love you so much."

There was a shout and sudden activity. Metal doors banged open, a metallic hum sounded, and the main aisle flooded with light. A new body filled the doorway and I flinched, then perked up when I recognized him. "Laurent?"

"Yeah, *chere*." The relaxed drawl of his Cajun dialect ... it made me want to cry. *He came to find me too.*

Laurent moved aside as two more men shouldered in. The three of them blocked the light from the hall and I had to squint to see their features in the dark. At the sight of Rick and Lance's pinched and concerned faces, I could no longer hold in the emotion. The pain, the exhaustion, the fear ... the relief of it all broke a dam in my heart. I lowered my forehead to Dario's chest and started to cry.

THE PRISONER

She swung open the door of the fourth cell, meeting the wary eyes of the blonde. The girl wasn't chained, her shackles removed months ago in exchange for her obedience. It was a shame. Given a little more time, she might have become something worthy. Instead, she'd be the ticket to Claudia's escape.

The blonde's gaze flicked to Claudia's shaved head, her eyes widening at the fresh haircut.

Claudia stepped inside and pointed the Taser. "Let's go."

The box had been installed first, the six-foot square cavity dug into the ground for the purpose of holding the fireproof box. An air pipe left the box and ran a quarter mile east, then came to the surface on the edge of a field. The warehouse had been built on top of the box, the entrance concealed in the concrete stairwell that led up to the second-floor office. Inside the box was a feed into the security cams and enough bottled water and provisions to support someone for several weeks, assuming they could deal with the boredom and the smell of their own excrement.

Robert's plan had always been simple. If the warehouse was discovered, if a threat came on property that was too big to overcome—get in the box and blow the place apart. Escape later, once the attention dies down.

The plan had always sucked, though she hadn't voiced that opinion to him. Now, she shoved the girl forward along the hall, out of the view of the other cells.

Entering the stairwell, she nodded toward the open hole in the ground, the box's interior dark, the blinking red lights of the security system giving an occasional blood-red peek. "Jump in." The girl hesitated and she pressed the Taser into her shoulder. "GO. Don't make me hurt you."

Back in the cell, she stripped off the T-shirt, then grabbed fistfuls of mud and rubbed it over her breasts and along her arms and the front of her jeans. She'd changed shortly after arriving and securing Bell Hartley. She'd washed off the clown makeup and ditched the Realtor costume, leaving the blonde wig on just in case. *Just in case* had been a good precaution, and the ratty jeans now worked well for her cause. She ran her dirty hands over her face and her shaved head, taking the oldest cell in the back and locking the ankle restraints into place. Her hands... she hesitated, and then left them free.

It had been four years since Robert first shackled her and Tanaka up in this exact same cell. Claudia had pulled at her restraints for weeks. Every girl in that place had only had one form of restraints, their wrists or ankles. She hadn't understood why, out of everyone there, he'd used *both* arm and leg restraints on her. When she'd earned her way out of the leg restraints, she'd cried. The arm restraints had taken so much longer. Tanaka had died before Claudia had been able to leave her place by the wall and move around freely, without the iron weight dragging her hands down.

Over three years had passed since her shackles had been removed, and she still couldn't have anything around her wrists. A bracelet, a watch, even a hairband caused her chest to tighten and her panic to swell. Now, she tested each ankles shackle, making sure they were convincingly secure. From a distance, one of the women called out, the sound echoing along the warehouse. Taking a deep breath, Claudia slid down the wall, her tailbone knocking painfully against the concrete floor, and brought her knees to her chest. They must be inside. They were probably creeping slowly through the building. *Looking for her*.

It was to her benefit that she'd spent those two days running from Robert. Skipping meals, torturing herself with guilt. In just days, her cheeks had thinned, her belly distended. Her muscles, developed from several years of strenuous workouts, had wilted.

She looked like death. Had felt like it. Earlier, when she'd lifted Bell Hartley over her shoulder to carry her out of the house, she'd struggled, the weight almost too much for her.

Close by, a footstep crunched. She immediately tensed, her arms wrapping around her knees, her face hidden behind her forearms. A man eased into the doorway, his head sweeping left to right, examining the small cell, and returned to her. She peeked out at him, and he lifted a finger, telling her to stay quiet.

She smiled, the gesture hidden behind her knees. *Idiot*.

TWENTY-SEVEN

THE RESCUED

Agent King peered at Claudia. "Name?"

She stayed quiet, picking incessantly at the sleeve of the long-sleeve shirt that someone had provided. Glancing around, her eyes picked up on all of the details. White walls. Cramped corners. A sterile scent that reeked of bleach. She'd kept her fingerprints to herself so far, pulling at the shirt sleeves and tucking her fists in them.

The other agent, a woman, leaned forward. She wore a name tag, one that said Marcantonio, though she'd told her to call her Gina— her tone the soothing sort typically reserved for toddlers. "Why did he shave your head?" She circled the edge of the table, peering at Claudia as if she was a window display. "None of the other women have shaved heads."

Claudia lifted her chin and met the woman's inquisitive stare. "Punishment."

That, paired with an irritated look from the head agent, shut her up. The woman folded her arms across her chest in an irritated fashion that made Claudia like her a little more. She stole a glance at the woman's watch and did the math. Fifty-four minutes had passed since she'd locked the blond in the box. Good thing she'd set the timer for an hour.

So far, in the half hour since they'd carefully brought her out of the cell, she'd been given a stack of Oreos and some water. She'd ignored half of their questions and given only short responses when she had responded. They hadn't pushed. They seemed to have the opinion that being kept prisoner weakened an individual's mental state. And maybe, in other camps and with other keepers, it did. But Robert Hawk was different. Under him, she had grown stronger—both mentally and physically. They were handling her with kid gloves when they should have brought out machetes.

She threw the first breadcrumb out. "How close are we to the warehouse?"

The agents exchanged a look, and the man responded. "About fifty feet."

She bound her hands across her midsection and glanced toward the door in her best impression of a nervous woman. "We should move."

The female agent got the hint, one she'd practically spray painted across the walls for them. "Why should we move?"

She didn't respond, taking the moment to begin rocking, her chin tucked, eyes down.

"Miss." He leaned forward, across the table, and when he reached a hand out toward her, she flinched as if she'd been shot. He retreated at the same time that the female agent advanced.

"Why do you want to be farther away from the warehouse?"

That was the thing about cops. Push them into the direction of a question, and then *don't* answer the question? They'd swarm on that topic like piranhas.

She swallowed, then threw them a giant, juicy bone. "I saw her, wiring the explosives." For theatrical fun, she took another fearful glance in the direction of the door, her rocking motion increasing in speed. "We should move further away."

Three minutes. Three minutes, and then it'd all be over with.

BELL

The moon swayed with each of Dario's steps. I gripped his neck and rested my head against his chest, listening to the solid beat of his heart. It didn't feel real, being reunited with him, being out of that place. I squeezed his neck muscles, inhaled the scent of him, and curled tighter into his hold.

"We're almost there. Just hold on."

I could see the ambulance ahead of us, its lights reflecting against his shirt, the doors open. An EMT ran beside Dario, trying to assist him, but I wouldn't let go of him, not until we got to the ambulance. They'd already prepped me for what would happen there: the removal of the knife. I was almost looking forward to it. The pain had dulled to a screaming throb, one that seemed to shriek with every step Dario took.

I squeezed his neck to get his attention. "Did they find the blonde? The one who took me?"

He looked down at me, and I watched his features harden. "Not yet. But don't worry, they will. That place is surrounded and the FBI just showed up. They'll get her, wherever she's hiding."

I nodded, my nerves bound tight. I watched the dark fields, the night enveloping us the moment we stepped away from the building. I needed them to find her. I needed her to be behind bars. I needed them to question her and find out what her motivations were, and why she was hell-bent on punishing us.

"Stop worrying. I'm here." His voice was gruff and his body curved around me, his mouth pressing a kiss against my forehead. I closed my eyes, my hand tightening on his arm.

"Tell me somewhere you've always wanted to go. Anywhere."

I looked up to find his gaze on me, the view bobbing as he carried me forward. "Anywhere?"

I had visited three states in my lifetime: Nevada, California, and now? Louisiana. Throw in a weekend trip to Tijuana once and I'd thought my world travels were over. "Alaska. I want to see a whale."

He chuckled. "Alaska it is. As soon as you're healed enough to travel."

His mouth returned to my head, then he strained down to reach my lips, the kiss a mix of desperation and need. He pulled away carefully, and I smiled.

"Don't forget the whale."

"I'll show you so many you'll grow bored of them."

There was a shout from behind us, the tones urgent. Dario spun around. The moon reflected off of the warehouse's metal roof, casting the rest of it in shadow, a long rectangle that looked too innocent, too peaceful. There was a long moment of quiet, and Dario started to turn back.

I stopped him. "Wait."

I pointed at the dark figures that streamed out of the warehouse door. The rescue team ran in all directions, some headed our way.

"What the—" Dario stepped back, shifting me higher for a better vantage point.

I turned my attention to the FBI trailer, watching as the door flew open, Agent King coming out, and turning to help a pair of women. The warehouse's door slowly swung shut, extinguishing the bright light of its interior, and cutting off my view of the ins—

Everything exploded in a flare of red hot heat. Debris flew, bits of dust and a force of wind hit my skin, and I ducked into Dario's chest, his hand cupping my head, his shoulder turning to shield us from the blast. We were across the field, yet I felt the vibration of it in my bones, the boom reverberating, the bright light of it blinding.

It was over in a heartbeat. Loud chaos, then the crackle of death. The heat retreated and I peered over his shoulder at what was left of the warehouse. It couldn't even be called that anymore. It was an inferno. Flames licked the sky, black smoke billowing, the bones of the building standing out in glowing red lines. Who had still been inside? With such a large building, with the teams looking for the kidnapper... *someone* had to have still been inside.

Someone...

I panicked, thinking of Rick... Lance... Laurent. I snapped my head to the left, then the right, scanning the dark fields, the paramedics, the bright orange glow of the fire. It reflected off the damaged trailer, the vehicles... I strained forward, fighting for a better view, and my leg screamed in protest.

"Miss—" The paramedic protested, and I waved him off.

"Where are—"

I saw Lance, crouched behind one of the prisoners, a cup in hand. I inhaled, my gaze jumping through the others, a windbreaker moving aside and revealing Rick, his arms crossed, attention on the flames. Unharmed. *Thank God.* I sagged into Dario's arms and felt his hands tighten on my legs.

"It's okay, Bell. I promise."

"Wait." I pushed against his chest, the final band of tension not yet released. "Where's Laurent?" I forced my gaze to slow, my eyes burning from the smoke, the glare still too intense to look at without squinting. I passed over paramedics, FBI jackets, and heavily armored men. I looked for a thick beard, for his beanie, for that huge build. "I can't find him!"

His hold tightened on me. "He's okay, Bell. He wasn't in there."

"No." I struggled in his hold, needing to be on my own feet, needing him to go there, right now, and *find* Laurent. He had to. I couldn't... if he... my chest constricted, my breath wheezing, and I dug my nails into his arm. "Dario, you have to find him. I CAN'T SEE HIM!"

I couldn't have another innocent death caused by our mistakes. Especially not Laurent. I thought of him, all of his gruff kindness, the way his eyes had squinted when he found something humorous, the way he had squeezed my shoulder in an attempt to comfort me. I clutched a fistful of Dario's shirt and shoved out of his arms, hobbling on one foot toward the paramedics. Dario followed, and I held up a hand and forced him to look in my eyes.

"Find him." I rasped out the order, my throat raw, my self-control wavering. "Please."

THE WINNER

She ran through the dark field, away from the police's entry points, aiming for the adjacent parcel. The grass was dry, the footing uneven, and she slowed her stride, her bare feet gingerly picking their way over the wild underbrush.

The urge to whoop out a victory call was tempting. Fuck the FBI. Fuck Bell Hartley and Dario Capece. Fuck every individual who thought that they could outsmart her. She was a mother-fucking Hawk. And soon, after the will was read, everyone would know it. She would get away with everything and Dario Capece would have no idea that his newest business partner was the same woman who had killed his wife.

Not that Gwen had been intentional. But hadn't Robert always said she was weak? Hadn't he taught Claudia lessons through Gwen's failures?

Sure, it hadn't fit their plan. She'd had big dreams of being best friends with Gwen. Equals. Sisters. That hadn't happened. What had Robert always said? *Pain makes us stronger*. Oh, and *death is part of life*. He'd told her that, right after he'd taken Tanaka's. Well, she had brought the death. Right now, Robert was watching her with a giant grin on his face. He was saying *well done* and bragging about the cunning daughter that he had. This plan was *better* than his plan. Or it would be, once she had a chance to change her appearance, create a new game plan, and come back into Dario Capece's life and finish the job.

He would never see her coming. Once the fire went out, once they found the eight-foot box with the blonde inside... their search for the kidnapping realtor would be over. Case closed. Danger gone.

She saw the fence ahead, the outline becoming visible in the dark. Slowing to a walk, she moved down its perimeter until she reached the gate, hidden from anyone who didn't know where to look. Picking up the lock, she entered the combination, yanked the latch open, then slipped through the opening.

Her vehicle was now gone, victim to the explosive devices that she and Robert had wired throughout the warehouse's infrastructure. It didn't matter. Stepping onto the neighboring parcel, she headed for the middle of the field and the small tree, planted specifically for one purpose—to mark the eight-foot box's air vent.

Before her, the sky glowed, the clouds reflecting the blaze, and the smell of smoke was heavy in the air. Slowing her steps, she scanned the ground, her search taking longer than expected before she found the small pipe, the diameter of a soda can.

"It looks too skinny." She examined the pipe, her opinion producing a scoff from Robert Hawk.

"Think of how small your throat is, little dove. You breathe just fine through it."

She wrapped her hands around her own throat, considering the logic. "How long would we survive without the air pipe?"

"In that box?" He frowned. "A half hour. Maybe less."

She crouched and lifted up the small cap that hung from the lip of the vent and twisted it on, tightly capping the vent and blocking the flow of fresh air.

She stood, taking a moment to look down at her handiwork and wondered if she would feel any compassion for the woman, trapped in that box, underneath that inferno. Ten seconds passed, and she envisioned what would happen when the air started to get thin, wondered if the box was properly insulating the woman from the heat. Another ten seconds passed, and she pictured her mounting panic, the desperate claw at the handle in an attempt to free herself. After another few seconds, she straightened, firm in her resolve and confident of her decision.

Maybe, she mused, she didn't have much of a heart left. Maybe, between Tanaka and Robert's death, there wasn't anything in her left to feel.

She thought back to Bell Hartley, remembered the way the

brunette's eyes had flashed when she'd said Dario's name. There had been fight in her little body, despite her weak position, the injection's drugs still present in her system. It'd been a cute letter. She'd seen the sincerity and thought behind it. She'd noticed the way her forehead had scrunched in concentration, the pen trembling when she'd put it to paper. The girl had stopped several times during the composition, pausing to think, putting the end of the pen in her mouth as she had reread over her last few lines.

Too bad the man had been Dario. With any other man, Claudia might have rooted her on. But Dario had already been taken, had been a pivotal part of the Hawk empire's success. Bell had threatened to take him away, a move that had jeopardized everything.

One little cocktail waitress, one Vegas slut out of a million...and she almost caused the fall of the Hawk dynasty. One little cocktail waitress, who caused a domino of events that had left both Gwen and Robert dead within a week of that San Diego trip.

Now, there was only herself. The last remaining Hawk, and the only daughter who was truly worthy of his bloodline. She had everything —the training, the self-control, the intelligence, the resolve. With her, the Hawk name would come back stronger than ever.

It wouldn't be easy. She'd have to be smart about it. Get plastic surgery. Lay low. Quietly work with Hawk's estate attorney to transfer his assets into her possession. Get her name changed. Wait several years and then reemerge and introduce herself to Vegas. To Dario. To Bell Hartley, should the weakling still be around.

They wouldn't recognize her. They'd welcome a long-lost Hawk with the proper level of courtesy and respect, especially with the business holdings that his estate would grant her. They'd bring her into their lives with no idea of the hell she would eventually unleash.

She turned back, the sound of sirens faint. Fire trucks. They wouldn't be able to do much. It'd take hours for the flames to die down. Hours for paperwork and investigations, for body counts and medical care. Would they even notice her absence? If they did, a half-hearted attempt to find the lost abducted girl might begin. But without a name, photo or suspicion of involvement, the search would wither, and the lost Hawk captive would eventually be a Wikipedia footnote and little else.

One girl gone. Another reborn.

She continued forward, and the sound of the highway grew louder. When the foot hooked around her ankle, she flew forward, her hands scraping on the rocks, and a scream slipped out of her before she could rein it in.

"Easy there." The voice was deep and unfamiliar, and she rolled to the side, scrambling to her feet, and froze at the sight of the man, her hands lifting, her eyes zeroing in on his gun.

"Who da fuck are you?" The man spoke with a thick drawl that dripped with an accent she couldn't place. He stepped closer, his face coming into focus, the moon exposing strong features almost hidden by a thick beard. He was a mountain man, one who yielded his gun with the confidence of someone interested in using it.

"And..." he smirked, settling into his stance, and nodded at the tree a hundred yards back. "What da fuck was that pipe?"

TWENTY-EIGHT

BELL

Hours. That was it. I was taken for only hours. Barely a quarter of a day, most of which I spent drooling on myself and unconscious to everything. Hours, yet I felt as if it changed my entire life.

I laid in the hospital bed, the room crowded with a constantly-changing mix of family and friends, and fought back tears. I smiled, I listened to their stories and prayers—but I only wanted him. I wanted him next to me in this skinny bed. I clutched his hand, drawn to the warmth of his skin, and wondered when he would have to leave.

The Dario I knew before had constantly worked. His phone had buzzed every few minutes, our time together stolen between meetings and calls, the twilight hours our only uninterrupted stretches. Now, I didn't even see his cell on him. He sat next to my bed, cradling my hand, and gave me his full focus. He brought me steak from S&L and chocolate chip cookies and milk from Patrizas. He noticed my shiver and hunted down, and then tucked a heated blanket around me. When my energy drooped, he ordered everyone out of the room, turned off the overhead light, and ran his hands through my hair until I fell asleep.

His full attention was temporary, I knew that. He had eight hotels to run, four casinos to control. Right now, crews were probably going wild without their captain. Soon, those lines etched in his brow would involve room rates and expense reports, turn figures and profitability ... and not just my health.

I took a deep breath, trying once again to not think about where I was and how I got here. "They need to let me out." I kicked my good leg free of the covers and growled in frustration. "My leg is fine." I had the brief memory of the woman, her foot hovering in the air above the knife. I flipped my gaze to Dario.

The corner of his mouth twitched into a smile. "You've got thirty-two stitches. Let's just give it another night."

It wasn't just the stitches. I knew that. He liked having me here, liked being able to see my heart rate and oxygen level with one easy glance. He touched me, frequently, as if to reassure himself that I was really here, and he drilled every doctor and nurse who stepped in the room as if they were on trial.

"This is a safe place. The best suite in the hospital. Be patient and let me pamper you."

Pamper wasn't the word I'd use. Everything had been a blur. I vaguely recalled a visit from the hospital president promising me whatever we needed. I wanted out. I wanted Dario. *I wanted the nightmare of her sadistic face erased from my head.*

"Until you feel up to house-hunting, I've had the staff at Vinente prepare the Presidential suite. It's four bedrooms, with a roof-top pool, and plenty of room to avoid me if I drive you—"

"That's fine." I carefully curled onto my side, facing him. "Anything is fine."

I didn't want to go back home. As much as I loved Meredith and the girls, as many memories as I had in that house, I was ready to leave. I needed some tranquility, and I needed him. I didn't care where we were, as long as we were together. Life was too precious to us right now. Too many deaths. Too much heartbreak. Too many lies and villainous acts. I wanted quiet and I wanted some space to grieve, because it would take a long time to work through what we've experienced. But with him, I knew I could—*we could*—heal.

He pulled my hand free of the blanket, cradling it between his palms before he brought it to his mouth and softly kissed the underside of my wrist.

"Can we go now? I got big plans for this bandage." I gestured to my leg, which seemed twice its normal diameter, given the generous swatch of bandages that circled it.

He chuckled and tugged gently on the end of my hair, which could use a thirty minute shower and half a bottle of shampoo. "Soon. Tomorrow."

I took the news with a nod, sinking back into the pillows. From the end of the room, the muted television screen caught my eye and I pointed, getting his attention. "Look. Turn this up."

On the screen was an aerial view of the warehouse, a cluster of equipment surrounding the charred infrastructure. And in the midst of the shot, the overhead camera flying low over the destroyed roofline, I saw the open trapdoor, surrounded by rubble, the view mostly obscured by the night. An FBI agent crouched by the entrance to the door, bending down into it. I sat further up in the bed, trying to get a better look. Dario found the remote and turned up the volume.

"The hidden compartment was discovered the next morning, the entrance door swelled shut due to the excessive heat of the fire. Incredibly enough, none of the interior was damaged by the fire. According to reports, this underground vault was actually fireproof, and designed as a safe room, for circumstances such as this one. While we haven't received confirmation, we believe that Janie Bostic, the twenty-three-year-old woman found inside this safe room, is one of Robert Hawk's victims. How or why she was protected in this horrific explosion? We hope to find out answers to that question soon. We do have confirmation that the woman was unharmed in the explosions and only being treated for minor injuries."

The woman took a dramatic pause, staring grimly into the camera while a mugshot appeared over her left shoulder. "An arrest has been made in the kidnapping of Bell Hartley. Claudia Vorherz allegedly posed as a real estate agent before drugging Hartley and taking her to Robert Hawk's warehouse. Interestingly enough, Claudia was one of the women originally believed to be one of Hawk's *victims*. We are waiting for an official statement from the FBI on the connection between her and Robert Hawk."

Dario glanced at me. "Talk about a clusterfuck. They don't know their asses from their elbows."

"They aren't too far off." It was a complicated mess of affairs we ourselves barely understood. Laurent had followed Claudia from the blaze and, after dragging her back to the FBI, had shown them the small pipe he'd watched Claudia visit during her escape. Forensic mapping of that air vent had led to the discovery of the safe room, and the woman inside.

I watched as the camera zoomed in on the front of the box. "This is exclusive footage, shot earlier, of rescue workers pulling Janie Bostic out of the eight-foot by eight-foot vault that almost became her tomb."

Music played and I watched as a thin woman was helped out of the hole, her long blond hair catching me off guard. I stole a glance at Dario, whose hand tightened around mine.

"She almost got away with it," I said quietly. "Killing and framing that girl." I would have believed it. A skinny woman with long blonde hair, tucked away in a fire-safe box, under an exploding building? She'd stayed in the shadows of the cell, and I hadn't paid enough attention to her at the house. If Claudia had been successful in blocking the airhole and suffocating Janie, I would have bought the 'accidental death' narrative. I would have gone to sleep thinking that our tormentor was dead. And she... she would have been out there, unchecked and still hell-bent on revenge. I thought of the steel tone of her voice, the threats she had spit out at me. *You don't get to love Dario Capece. And he doesn't get to fuck around without having serious consequences brought down on his shoulders.*

I would never have put the pieces together myself. With the drugs, the pain, my surgery ... it had taken me every minute of the last two days just to become coherent. Laurent had been the one to follow Claudia to the station, and keep us abreast of the updates. While she had refused to say anything in the questioning, they'd managed to piece together enough details to create a narrative.

I didn't need her confession. I could still hear her voice in my mind, threatening me with quiet confidence. A shiver went through me, and I pulled my blanket higher on my chest.

Dario's pocket hummed and he reached in and brought out his cell. "It's the detective. I need to take this."

I nodded and relaxed back in the bed, watching the television, the broadcasts giving us a colorful spread of Instagram photos that looked nothing like the cold-hearted bitch who had almost stomped a knife through my leg. Claudia had disappeared two years ago, and the photos were all pre-abduction. Claudia, in a nurse's Halloween costume, making a hang ten sign and sticking out her tongue. Claudia, hugging a giant Rottweiler, sunglasses on, her hair in knots on either side of her head. Claudia, with a group of blurred out faces, outside a club.

I had been in that warehouse for a half-dozen-hours. Claudia had been gone for two years. How could I say what that sort of time did to someone? How could *any* of us understand the atrocities that must have happened to her to change her from a normal girl to a monster?

I watched a new addition to the show, an opinionated reporter who spewed theories. Vegas Suites had been one of Hawk's properties, acquired the summer before Claudia disappeared. She'd been a front desk agent, and had been known to be a party girl, one who experimented in drugs when she wasn't working.

Somehow, the news about Dario and my affair hadn't hit the press. My kidnapping was being viewed in the same thread as the other victims—the snatch of a young woman who could be trained to do Hawk's biding.

The reporter pointed to the camera, his voice growing emphatic.

"Imagine the level of brainwashing that Robert Hawk was capable of. He takes Claudia Vorherz out of her daily life—imprisons her—and then has her, less than two years later, doing his hunting for him and continuing his legacy, even after he's gone!"

He spread his palms and looked at his cohost.

"Think about *that*. We're talking about our generation's Charles Manson. Claudia Vorherz blew up that warehouse without *any* knowledge of who was still inside. She detonated that structure and could have possibly killed a dozen law enforcement officers, not to mention the remaining prisoners—women just like her—and she did it anyway. Burned the place to the ground with no concern over human casualties, and with her primary focus being on framing Janie Bostic for her crimes. If she didn't learn that directly from the evil that is Robert Hawk, you tell me where she learned it. Because I'm *damn* sure she didn't learn it slinging back beers with her friends..."

The anchors chatted on, but I couldn't listen to them any more. I reached for the remote and muted the volume. Closing my eyes, I tried to rest my mind. I could do this. One day at a time.

Dario came back in and turned off the lamp. "Her hearing is tomorrow. She still hasn't said anything." He folded down the railing on the side of my bed.

I raised my eyebrows at him with a laugh. "What are you doing?"

"Scoot over." He gently nudged me over to the edge of the bed, the thin mattress sinking as he climbed onto it.

I laughed harder as his elbow knocked over my juice box, his leg getting tangled in the remote cord, his exasperation growing. Then he was pulling me to him, his body curving around mine, and the fit, with us front to back on our sides, was perfect. I relaxed, my mind pulling away from the reporter's emphatic statements and focused on the deep sounds of his breathing, the soft nuzzle of his mouth against the back of my neck.

"What are you thinking about?" he asked.

I shifted, moving closer to him. "I'm just worried that we'll never get away from her. With all of the businesses Gwen owned with her father—businesses that you now own? How will that work, if Claudia inherits his piece of them?"

He carefully sat up, rolling me onto my back so that he could see my face. "I don't want you to worry about that, about her. She's in jail. She's going to be in prison, for a very long time. I've got everybody I know working to guarantee that."

"But one day, she'll get out." I met his eyes.

"And we will be fine when she does." He leaned forward and gently kissed me. When he pulled away, his face was solemn. "Please believe me when I promise you that it will be okay. I will keep you safe. Us safe. I swear."

I sighed. "I believe you." I softened under his second kiss, then settled back on my side, his body returning into place, the warm comfort solidifying my trust in him.

"Don't give up on us," he said softly, and the request surprised me. We'd survived. Hawk. Claudia. Everything. Giving up? Running? That was the last thing on my mind.

Love me through the cracks.

I pulled his arms tighter around me. "Never."

TWENTY-NINE

ONE WEEK LATER

DARIO

She rolled over in bed and stretched, his white t-shirt huge on her, her dark hair tickling his bicep. He gathered her into his chest and she curled against him, one leg thrown over his, the gauze of her bandage brushing against him. She winced, and he carefully eased her higher, into a position that was better for the wound.

He couldn't look at it without wanting to kill Claudia Vorherz. Jail was too good for her. For all they knew, she had been the one to kill Gwen. She could have called her to the suite, posed in a brunette wig as Bell, then shot her the minute that Gwen turned her back.

"You look so serious." Bell said, and he lifted his gaze to hers. She smiled and his anger at Claudia, a woman who would spend the next decade behind bars, faded. Bell's smile did unnatural things to him. Her voice, still husky with sleep, brought his arousal to life.

He redirected his thoughts away from anything sexual and pressed a soft kiss to her forehead. "Good morning."

She yawned, the gesture so big that he could see a filling peek out from one of her molars. "Good morning."

"How are you feeling?"

She thought about the question for a beat. "I'm starving."

"But, no pain?"

She made a face. "Nothing too bad. Got time for breakfast before you leave?"

He winced at the thought of going to his office, diving back into the thick of things. Being away for a week would mean massive issues. In the hospitality business, you had to be continually vigilant or you might as well give up.

He kissed her. "I'll always have time for breakfast for you."

She smiled again, and a part of his broken heart healed.

THE INMATE

Claudia yawned and listened to Bertha. The woman had an issue. Her brother's girlfriend was pregnant, that skank slept with half the mother-fuckin' city, and because she'd been kissing up to him the last two weeks, he thought the baby was his, and was going to put his name on the birth certificate when it came.

It'd been four days since her brother had called and the issue hadn't changed. Bertha sat on that stupid cot all day and obsessed over it. She didn't understand. The more anger you gave someone, the more power they had over you. The more obsessed you grew, the more vulnerable that obsession made you.

Claudia had learned that lesson the hard way. It was why she was sitting here, a number stitched across her right breast. *She* had obsessed. *Robert* had obsessed. They had both let emotions dictate actions and it had led to this.

It was a new day. Going forward, everything would be done the *right* way. She would take the lessons that Robert Hawk had taught her, analyze their potential, and learn from his mistakes. Her father wasn't a God. Her sister wasn't a saint. Claudia wasn't infallible.

"It just ain't right." Bertha shook her head. "You know she gonna get child support out of this. Eighteen years' worth. And he ain't got a pot to piss in."

Claudia tuned the woman out. Ninety women in this detention center, and she had gotten lucky with Bertha. Some of these bitches were crazy. Bertha was just dumb.

She opened the notebook and flipped through the pages the attorney had given her, scanning the long list of assets. Robert Hawk had been very generous to his two daughters. Given the untimely death of Gwen, Gwen's portion had automatically fallen to her.

Four hundred and three million dollars' worth of assets. She circled the ones she wanted to keep and starred the items that could be sold. Her eyes drifted over the values and she contemplated what to do with all of that money.

The answer, of course, was easy. First, get her freedom. Then, ruin Bell and Dario's lives.

Getting her freedom would require some patience. The best legal team money could buy. Expert psych consultants who would attest to her temporary insanity. A well-negotiated plea deal that would reduce her kidnapping and attempted murder charges down to the minimum sentencing standards. Sure, she'd spend time in prison. Eight to ten years at minimum, according to her attorneys. She did, after all, aid in the imprisonment and torture of nine women. She did, after all, kidnap Bell Hartley with intent to kill, then stuffed Janie Bostic in that little concrete vault with plans to suffocate her to death. The evidence, in all of those charges, was irrefutable.

But no one knew about Gwen. They suspected, they had accused, but there was no evidence. Nothing linking her to the crime. *Nothing.*

So, she'd avoided a murder charge. And for the other stuff, she'd get a new home in a comfortable prison. Maybe even a posh psych ward, though there wasn't a more lucid mind than hers within a thousand miles.

And after a few years, with perfect behavior and annual appeals, she'd be paroled. *Free.* Free and filthy rich. Free and well prepared to ruin Bell and Dario's lives.

She closed the notebook and sat back on the cot, hugging the book to her chest and smiling.

She didn't even mind the wait. It would give her more time to calmly, coolly, and intelligently prepare. This would not be like before. This time, she would make no mistakes.

BELL

The hotel was at the quiet end of the city, our suite facing the city. I wore one of Dario's shirts, the scent of him surrounding me, and stood on the balcony. From this spot, I could see the Majestic, see the tiny dark roof of The House. I heard the faint sound of a coyote, its cry joined by another, then a chorus of soft howls. I felt the tickle of cold air and turned my head, seeing Dario step out, his arms wrapping around my waist.

"Pretty view," I commented.

"It's not what I'm looking at."

I turned in his arms, facing him. Looking into his face, I gently traced over his features. "You look stressed."

"I'm not. Not anymore." He leaned forward and kissed me tenderly, taking his time with it. When he pulled away, I could tell that he had something on his mind. "I hired a CEO today."

"Really?" I reached up and worked at the knot of his tie, loosening it. "What does that mean?"

"It means that I am, officially, stepping away from work."

My fingers stilled. "Is that what you want?"

"I want to spend my time with you. This summer, before you go back to school, or work, or whatever you choose to do..." He leaned forward and stole another kiss. "I want to be here. With you. I don't want to waste two months looking at fucking revenue reports and a casino floor."

I smiled at the thought. "What will we do all summer?"

"I was thinking about that," he said soberly, his brow pinching in mock concentration. "We have a jet. A ridiculously fat bank account. Strict orders from your doctors to have as much sex as humanly possible."

I laughed and tugged at his tie, getting it loose. "That's not what I remember them saying."

His mouth twitched and he ran his hands up my side, gathering me closer to him. "I thought we'd find a place to live, somewhere without an elevator and parking garage."

"That sounds good..." I mused, undoing the top button of his dress shirt.

"And get you on a beach. Somewhere with turquoise water and a frozen drink. Poolside massages and private butlers."

I leaned forward and nipped his neck. "And Alaska," I reminded him.

"God yes. Are you kidding? Whales everywhere."

I giggled. "That sounds good to me. But no travel right away." I tugged on his shirt. "This ... time with you... that's all I want."

He kissed me softly, then deeper, and the air changed. I dug my fingers in his hair, fought his kiss with my mouth, and didn't hesitate when he pulled away from me and spoke.

"Turn around and spread your feet apart."

I felt his shoe nudge my inner calf and I acquiesced, letting out a soft exhale when he undid my shirt, skimming the stiff fabric over my shoulders and dropping it to the floor.

"Jesus Christ, you're beautiful. Stay just like that."

He crouched behind me, running his hands up my inner thighs, one gripping my left ass cheek, the other gently running in between my legs, his fingers playing over and teasing the sensitive flesh there. I sighed out a protest, even as my legs widened, my hands tightening on the railing. Bare against the night breeze, my nipples stood at attention, and when he pushed a finger inside, I groaned.

"How gentle do I need to be with you?" He bit the back of my leg and I ignored it, his finger starting to pulse in and out of me, his knuckles brushing against my clit with every consistent swipe.

I pushed my ass out, resting my breasts against the railing. "Not gentle."

He didn't change anything, letting me adapt to the touch, his finger continuing to piston in and out of me, the pleasure building. I moved minutely, brushing the hard pebbles of my nipples along the railing, the cool metal a delicious contrast against the evening heat.

"Take your time. Enjoy it."

I didn't want to take my time. It was coming, my pussy clenching around his finger, my clit growing heavy and needy, crying out with each brush of contact. I rocked my torso more aggressively, closing my eyes and imagining the railing as a mouth, one on each breast, tongues flicking across the pink tips. He bit me again, and I broke.

The orgasm cascaded, tremors rocking me, my bud of arousal pulsing with the waves of pleasure. I gasped my way through it, clinging to the railing for support, my legs growing weak, his fingers never slowing, not until every sensation had passed and I reached back, pushing him away.

He stood, and I turned, stumbling toward him, the tent visible in his pants. Bending slightly, he gripped my ass and lifted me into the air, my legs wrapping around his waist, and he carried me inside, carefully setting me on the middle of the bed.

Then, he wasn't gentle. He wasn't rough. He was perfect.

I laid in bed and listened to the shallow sounds of his breathing, my eyes moving over the luxurious room, so much nicer than anything I ever expected to have in life. I rolled on one side and stared at him, examining his handsome features. The slightly crooked nose. Thick lashes. Strong brow. Full lips. Behind those lashes, were eyes that studied me as if memorizing me. Those lips had uttered words that had brought me arousal, laughter and security. Behind that brow was a calculating mind that had restored an empire and chosen me despite all of the reasons to run.

I pulled the sheet down, moving closer to him and placing my hand on his chest. Underneath my palm beat a heart that loved more fiercely than I thought possible. A heart that protected those he loved and spoiled me with every beat and chance. I ran my hand over his chest, over a scar that had come from a fight as a Louisiana boy, and moved closer, his arm reaching out, pulling me into his body.

Even in sleep, he desired me. Even in sleep, I felt safe in his arms. I closed my eyes and tucked more tightly into his embrace, allowing myself to fall asleep.

EPILOGUE

TWO MONTHS LATER

The sun was low in the sky when the first whale breached. I gasped, gripping Dario's bicep and pointed toward it. He smiled down at me, then followed my finger, the whale's tail tipping into the air before he settled softly into the water.

Dario's fingers linked with mine and he pulled me back against his chest, his chin resting on my head. I lifted my camera and waited, scanning the horizon for another one.

He squeezed and then released me. "They have photographers. You can just watch."

I waved him off, my stomach pressed to the railing, eyes pinned to the waves.

"Look, a baby." He pointed to the right and I stood on my toes, swooning a little at the miniature body that crested the surface.

It was incredible. More than I thought it would be. The crisp air, the sounds, the gorgeous canvas. I sighed happily and glanced over to catch him watching me, a small smile on his face.

"I'm so lucky to have you."

I scoffed, blushing as I looped my arm through his and rested my head on his shoulder. "Stop. I'm the lucky one."

"Thank you for dragging me here."

I laughed. It hadn't exactly been easy. He'd booked the tickets and the cruise immediately. But hours before our flight, a pipe had burst in the kitchen of Fat Clemenzas and flooded the slot floor of Ja-Nule. I'd had to rip the phone from his hand and threaten to throw it off the balcony if he didn't let his managers do their jobs and head to the airport with me. "I'm sure it won't be the last time I have to toss threats in order to get you on a vacation."

"Threaten away." He pressed his lips to my head. "I love you."

The crowd surged to the front of the boat, something spotted, but I didn't move, lifting my chin up to him for a kiss. He lowered his mouth to mine, and in the background, I heard the cry of a whale's song.

The restaurant took up the north end of the boat, our view all stars and blue ocean. Dario swirled the bubbly liquid around in the flute, then set it down, meeting my eyes. "Do you know when I first knew?"

"Knew what?" I licked the last bit of chocolate off the fork, then set it down.

"That I was in love with you."

I leaned forward, my forearms digging into the tablecloth. "When?"

"Outside your work. Right after you interrupted my conference call by wrapping your hand around my cock."

"Oh god." I rolled my eyes. "Really? That's when you fell for me?"

"Not then." He lifted his glass and took a sip. "It was when you walked away from me. You told me that you didn't need me and you walked away, without looking back." He set down the glass and leaned forward. "And it fucking *broke* me. I was left in that car, my dick half hard, my life—which had seemed pretty fucking great three weeks earlier—a pile of bullshit, and I wanted you back. And I knew, right then, that you were different. I knew that if I continued chasing you, continued hunting down a relationship with you ... that it wouldn't be one that I could recover from. I had to decide, right then, if you were going to be just another fling or if you were going to be my future."

I propped my chin in one hand and thought back on that night, on how conflicted I'd felt when I'd walked away from him. I remember the rest of that night, how I had been so torn over what to do. I remember thinking that we had something special, but that we were also once-in-a-lifetime levels of fucked up. Now, we felt anything but fucked-up.

I grabbed his hand. "I'm glad you didn't give up on me. I'm glad we didn't turn into just a fling."

It still felt almost wrong to say that. With all that had happened, I still struggled to feel as if we deserved a happy ending. It was something I discussed with my psychiatrist, something both of us were working to forget. But this trip, this moment ... we were moving in the right direction. He kissed my hand and smiled at me.

"There was never a chance of that. Not with us."

I lifted my glass in a toast. "To flings becoming more."

He smirked. "To flings becoming love."

Our flutes gently clinked together.

Beside us, a glacier slowly came into view, the white mountain dwarfing the boat. I nodded to it. "It makes me feel so small."

"Yeah." He watched it go by, and a moment of silence fell.

I toyed with my napkin, folding it in half before looking up. "I think you should go back to work."

He tilted his head at me as if confused. "I am—"

"No." I shook my head. "You're not. You're working a little but you're not running everything." I met his eyes. "And I think it's driving you crazy."

He sighed. "I told you I'd work less. Delegate more. The new CEO is doing fine. He—"

"He's not you." I'd seen the dark shadow that passed over Dario when he read the CEO's weekly report. It would put him in a funk the entire afternoon. I'd listened in as he'd go behind the man's back, get updates from middle managers, and quietly put out fires he couldn't help but get involved in. I'd felt the restlessness in him in the evenings, his workout regime become almost fanatical in its energy-burning attempts.

"I told you I would protect you. Support you. Actually be in a relationship with you." He lifted one shoulder. "How much of a relationship can we be in if I work all the time?"

"You worked all the time when we met. You worked all the time *and* had Gwen." I hated to say her name, hated to bring her up, but we couldn't pretend like she never existed. Not when her foundation was rebuilding schools in Vegas, her name popping up on libraries, her grants helping small businesses everywhere. She deserved to have a place in our history and our presence. Still, his face tightened at her name, his pain still present at her absence.

I reached across the table and picked up his hand. "I don't need you constantly. I just need stolen moments. I need to have you next to me at some point in the night. I need you to be happy and I don't want to be the only thing in your life that makes you that way."

His fingers tightened on mine. "I don't want to lose you."

I smiled. "You'll never lose me. Plus, starting next week, I'm going to be busy with school."

"Oh, God." He groaned. "Just promise, once you learn all the secrets of the human brain, you won't psychoanalyze me."

I made a face. "Are you kidding? You're going to be my pin cushion. Everything up there?" I reached up and drummed my fingertips on his forehead. "It's gold."

I had decided, after thrice-weekly sessions with the most expensive shrink Dario could find, that I want to be a psychiatrist. One like Dr. Anders. The woman was incredible, and if I'd had her as a teenage girl, after my rape? I may have become an entirely different woman. Not that I wasn't happy with the way my life had turned out. But she was a master at helping me see the big picture, at understanding my feelings and motivations, and at healing the pain that I still carried from that night.

Together, we'd been working through my guilt over Gwen, and I'd felt so much better after our first few weeks, I'd practically tied Dario to her chair and forced him to speak to her.

He was less enthusiastic than me at the concept of therapy. But he kept seeing her. And over the last two months, I'd seen the impact of her sessions in his own gradual peace.

I wanted to be her. I wanted to help people. Heal people. I wanted to work with abused and raped teenagers, trauma victims, and families of alcoholics. I wanted to make a difference, and the idea and possibility of that filled me with such purpose, such happiness, that I had all but somersaulted into my advisor's office with the paperwork to change my major.

He shifted, his gaze on the glacier, and I didn't need six years of med school to know that he was itching to take my directive and go back to work.

"Just do it." I nudged him with my foot. "When we get back, demote or fire that CEO, and take the reins back. It's what you were born to do."

"No." He shook his head. "I was born to love you."

My heart skipped at the look in his eyes, the sincere way he delivered the words. They were a promise.

"But..." he gave me a playful grin. "I think you're right. I'm going fucking mad with not knowing everything. With feeling as if I don't have control of the businesses." He studied me for a long moment. "You know, in a heartbeat, I could leave it. If you become unhappy, if I seem detached—"

"STOP." I grinned. "Stop." I leaned across the table and gently stole a kiss. "I brought it up because I meant it. Now stop hemming and hawing and just tell me you'll do it."

He chuckled and lifted his champagne glass in a second toast. "To doing what, and *who*, we were born to do." He winked at me, and I met his toast with a laugh.

"Cheers to that."

I was taking my sip when he stood, holding out a hand and nodding to the open deck of the ship, where a band played under the stars.

"I haven't danced since I was a teenager, drunk and idiotic at a fais-do-do. But if you aren't too embarrassed, I'd love to have this dance."

I stood, taking his hand and letting him pull me onto the floor, a Frank Sinatra song floating softly from the bandstand. "What's a fais-do-do?"

He spun me, then pulled me close, his hand settling on my waist with the practiced ease of a bullshitter.

"It's a Cajun dance party. Very sophisticated affair. Lots of liquor and shouting at each other. I'll take you back to Louisiana and let you get me drunk, you can see it all in action."

I smiled, loving the idea of the chance to see Laurent and Septime. "I'd like that. You can show me all of your old stomping grounds."

"I could take you frogging," he suggested, and I grimaced. He laughed, and spun me around before bringing me back in. "Okay," he amended. "No frogging. But I do need to roughen you up a little. You can't date a man from Louisiana and be afraid to get a little dirty."

I snorted. "I think we've established that I can be *very* dirty."

His smile widened and he pulled me in closer, cradling my face and lowering his mouth to mine for a kiss. And there, under the Alaskan sky, with a glacier the size of a skyscraper floating beside us, I fell a little deeper in love.

Want to read into another Alessandra Torre novel? Keep flipping the pages to see a few recommendations.

Want updates, sneak peeks, exclusive giveaways and more? Join over 40,000 readers and enroll in Alessandra's free monthly newsletter! Visit NextNovel.com to enroll.

LOOKING FOR ANOTHER BOOK TO READ?

My books vary in genre, so no matter what you are in the mood for, there is sure to be something that fits your need. Please see below for a list of some of my popular novels, organized by genre. Everything listed is a standalone, unless otherwise notated. Happy reading!

Romantic Suspense:

Moonshot, the New York Times Bestseller. Baseball's hottest player has his eye on only one thing—his team's 18-year-old ballgirl. Their forbidden relationship turns deadly when young women start dying.

The Girl in 6E. (First in a standalone series) A sexy internet superstar hides a dark secret: she's a reclusive psychopath.

Non-Romantic Psychological Suspense:

The Ghostwriter. Famous novelist Helena Roth is hiding a dark secret – her perfect life is a perfect lie. Now, as death approaches, she must confess her secrets before it's too late. An emotional and suspense-charged novel.

Sexy Romance:

Hidden Seams. A billion-dollar fashion empire is surrounded by secrets, sex and lies.

Hollywood Dirt. (Now a Full-length Movie!) When Hollywood comes to a small town, sparks fly between its biggest star and a small-town outcast.

Blindfolded Innocence. (First in a series) A college student catches the eye of Brad DeLuca, a divorce attorney with a sexy reputation that screams trouble.

Black Lies, the New York Times Bestseller. A love triangle with a twist that readers couldn't stop talking about. You'll hate this heroine until the moment you love her.

Love, Chloe. (First created for Cosmpolitan.com) A fallen socialite works for an heiress, dodges an ex, and juggles single life in the city that never sleeps.

ABOUT THE AUTHOR

Alessandra Torre is an award-winning New York Times bestselling author of seventeen novels. Torre has been featured in such publications as Elle and Elle UK, as well as guest blogged for the Huffington Post and RT Book Reviews. She is also the Bedroom Blogger for Cosmopolitan.com. In addition to writing, Alessandra is the creator of Alessandra Torre Ink, a website, community, and online school for aspiring authors.

Learn more about Alessandra at alessandratorre.com or join 40,000 readers and sign up for her popular monthly newsletter at nextnovel.com.

CPSIA information can be obtained
at www.ICGtesting.com
Printed in the USA
LVHW03s2217040818
585976LV00001B/94/P

9 780999 784150